Moira waited un~~til~~
before getting up ~~to lock the door.~~

This next conversation needed to be private. When she turned back around, Titus was once again leaning against the counter with his arms crossed over his chest, doing his best to look relaxed. However, she'd learned a lot about reading body language over the course of her career. To a casual observer, Titus might look cool, calm and collected, but there was a lot of tension in his shoulders and panic in the depths of those deep brown eyes.

Positioning herself a few feet in front of him, she met his gaze head-on. "Ordinarily I would now ask how you happen to know about my allergies. But all things considered, I don't have to, seeing as you're not Titus Kondrat at all."

She prowled a few steps closer, a mix of anger and betrayal feeding her fury. "So tell me, Ryan Donovan, how long have you been out of prison?"

Dear Reader,

All of my books are special to me, but I am really excited about the release of the third book in my Heroes of Dunbar Mountain series. Every so often, a particular character comes along who is extra special and becomes incredibly real to me. They magically step out of the shadows of my imagination and demand to have their story told and very much on their terms.

Titus Kondrat, the hero in *Second Chance Deputy*, is definitely one of those. When I first started populating the town of Dunbar, my intent was to use Titus as one of the background characters. Boy, that sure didn't last long, because somehow he ended up playing pivotal roles in both of the earlier books in the series.

Even so, Titus remained a man with many secrets and a past that he still hadn't come to terms with. Enter Officer Moira Fraser, the only woman he's ever loved and the newest member of the Dunbar Police Department. Needless to say, things get interesting after that.

I hope you enjoy getting to know Titus and Moira as they deal with the problems of their shared past and the possibilities of a new future together.

Happy reading,

Alexis

HEARTWARMING

Second Chance Deputy

—

Alexis Morgan

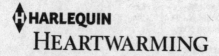

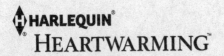

HARLEQUIN®
HEARTWARMING™

ISBN-13: 978-1-335-47558-9

Second Chance Deputy

Copyright © 2023 by Patricia L. Pritchard

Recycling programs
for this product may
not exist in your area.

For questions and comments about the quality of this book,
please contact us at CustomerService@Harlequin.com.

Harlequin Enterprises ULC
22 Adelaide St. West, 41st Floor
Toronto, Ontario M5H 4E3, Canada
www.Harlequin.com

Printed in U.S.A.

USA TODAY bestselling author **Alexis Morgan** has always loved reading and now spends her days creating worlds filled with strong heroes and gutsy heroines. She is the author of over fifty novels, novellas and short stories that span a wide variety of genres: American West historicals; paranormal and fantasy romances; cozy mysteries; and contemporary romances. More information about her books can be found on her website, alexismorgan.com.

Books by Alexis Morgan

Harlequin Heartwarming

Heroes of Dunbar Mountain

The Lawman's Promise
To Trust a Hero

Love Inspired The Protectors

The Reluctant Guardian

Visit the Author Profile page
at Harlequin.com for more titles.

This book is dedicated to my friend and brainstorming partner, Janice Kay Johnson. We've plotted an awful lot of books together over the years, and it never gets any less fun. I am grateful every day for her friendship and amazing creativity.

CHAPTER ONE

IT HAD BEEN an uneventful shift so far, especially for a Saturday night. Knowing that could change at any moment, Moira Fraser savored the quiet while it lasted. For now, she slowly steered her cruiser through the heart of town toward the church where Cade Peters, her boss and the chief of police, had just married Shelby Michaels. While Cade was relatively new to the area, Shelby and Moira had both grown up in the small town.

The difference was that Shelby had never left while Moira had only recently moved back after spending fourteen years living in Seattle. The city was only about one hundred and thirty miles from Dunbar, but it was a world away in size and intensity. She'd moved there to go to college, where her mother had expected her to get a teaching certificate and then hustle right back home. In a rare show of rebellion, Moira had majored in criminal justice, put on a police uniform and launched her career in law enforcement.

She'd loved her job in the big city and had been told she stood a good shot at moving up the ranks. While Moira had sometimes missed life in a small town, career opportunities in law enforcement in a place the size of Dunbar were extremely limited. Besides, the prior chief of police in town had been old-school, with no interest in hiring a female officer.

When she'd had to move back to town because her family needed her help, Moira had no idea what kind of job she'd be able to find. Fortunately, Cade Peters didn't share his predecessor's prejudices and immediately hired her, something she'd always be grateful for. To everyone's surprise—including hers— he'd also put her in charge of the small police force for the three weeks he would be away on his honeymoon. She'd heard rumblings that some members of the city council hadn't approved of his decision, but Cade had stood his ground.

One way or the other, she would justify his faith in her. She'd told him that one last time when she'd put in a brief appearance at the reception before resuming her patrol.

The church was now in sight, and she'd timed her arrival perfectly. The wedding guests stood clustered around the front steps as the bride and groom prepared to make their escape. Cade and Shelby held hands and laughed as they ran for the waiting limousine, passing by their friends and relatives, who stood on both sides waving colorful flags.

As the happy couple sped away to start their life together, Moira wondered if anyone had been able to find out where they would be spending their honeymoon. There had been a betting pool about the possible destinations. The suggestions ran the full gamut from the ridiculous to the sublime. Moira had five dollars riding on a Caribbean cruise, but she didn't care if she won. She just wanted her boss and his bride to have a solid three weeks of fun and relaxation without interference from anyone. It was still hard to believe that the city council had actually tried to order the newlyweds to go no farther away than nearby Seattle in case they needed Cade to come back early. She could only imagine how well that had gone over with him.

The crowd was rapidly dispersing, which meant it was time for her to get back to work. She resumed patrolling, taking her time as she circled the center of town again before gradually making her way to the outlying areas. Watching over her friends and neighbors was her favorite part of the job. She liked to think they slept better knowing someone was keeping an eye on things.

Still, she couldn't help but regret that she hadn't been able to spend more time at the reception. Since moving back to town two months ago, she had been working hard to reconnect with old friends, and Shelby had been one of the first to reach out to her. Unsurprisingly, Shelby had been too busy to spend a lot of time with any one guest at the reception. Even so, she and Cade made a valiant effort to personally greet everyone, especially those who'd come to town on such short notice. However, there were a few other people that Moira would've enjoyed hanging out with for longer than the half hour she'd been there.

Interestingly, there had been one person she'd expected to see but who had been missing in action—Titus Kondrat, the owner of the only café in Dunbar. Considering he'd been responsible for much of the excellent dessert buffet at the reception, it seemed odd that the man himself had been nowhere to be found. Not that she'd wanted to actually talk to him, but she made a habit of keeping a wary eye on him from a distance whenever she had the chance.

Oddly enough, from what she could tell, the police chief and Titus had become pretty good friends since Cade had moved to Dunbar. The two men seemed an odd match considering Cade was a by-the-book cop and Titus was… Well, that was an interesting question to ponder as she drove through the darkness. No one knew much about him since the man was amazingly closemouthed about his past.

Granted, people were entitled to their privacy, but for some reason that man set off Moira's Spidey-senses. They'd never actually spoken, but there was something familiar about him, most likely because he reminded her of a few criminals she'd helped put behind bars. The image of one guy in particular being led away in cuffs leaped to mind, but she refused to think about him right now.

After nearly ten years, the memory still hurt. She couldn't picture Cade being best buddies with someone who might have flirted with the wrong side of the law, but there was just something about Titus that didn't add up quite right. That was a mystery to mull over another day, though. For now, she'd make another loop through town and then stop in at the office to check on a few things. Cade had told her to leave all the paperwork for him to deal with upon his return. Even so, she planned to make sure that she and the other officers kept on top of everything so the boss didn't return to a huge backlog of work. It would be easy to let things slide, but that wasn't happening on her watch.

As she turned back toward the police station, her phone rang. One look at the name on the screen and she couldn't help but sigh. No matter how many times Moira told her mother not to call when she was on duty unless it was an emergency, the message never got through. She could be calling because there was a real problem, but it was just as likely that she wanted Moira to pick up milk on her way home. She hoped that wasn't the case. There wasn't a store in Dunbar that stayed open past nine, and she didn't want to drive the twenty miles to the nearest gas station with a mini-mart.

She put the call on speakerphone so she could keep both hands on the wheel. "What's up, Mom?"

"I'm sorry, hon, but Gram slipped away again. I'm heading out to search for her, but I might need your help getting her back home."

"I'm on my way. I'll drive by her house first."

"Sorry. I know you don't like to be bothered at work."

"Don't worry about it, Mom. Besides, it's part of the job—I'd do the same for anyone. I'll text or call as soon as I have news."

"I appreciate it."

Her poor mother sounded exhausted, mainly because she probably was. Taking care of Moira's elderly grandmother 24/7 wasn't easy. It was the reason Moira had moved back home, but there was a limited amount of support she could offer her mom. Between her time on the job and the need to sleep occasionally, there weren't many hours left over to spend standing watch over her grandmother.

Two blocks later, she turned down the street where her grandmother had lived for most of her life. More and more Gram's mind got tangled up in the past. When that happened, she forgot that she now lived with her daughter and granddaughter, and would try to go back home. At least the old place was currently vacant, so she wouldn't be bothering anyone when she started knocking on the door trying to get in.

Moira could only hope that was where her grandmother had gone this time. Otherwise, they could be in for a long night of driving up and down every street in town looking for her. Thankfully, most folks in Dunbar knew Gram. If she was spotted, whoever found her would do their best to contain Gram until either Moira or her mother came to take her back home.

Ten minutes later, her phone rang again. She answered without looking at the number. "Mom? Did you find her?"

A rusty laugh was followed by "I'm pretty sure I'm the wrong gender to be your mom, Officer Fraser."

Next time she vowed to check the caller ID before answering. Besides, why on earth would Titus Kondrat be calling her? "Sorry about that, Mr. Kondrat. How may I help you?"

"I'm at the café. I believe I have your grandmother sitting in my kitchen drinking a cup of tea and eating a piece of cherry pie."

Could this get any worse? Of all people to find Gram, it had to be him. Not that she wasn't grateful. "I'll be right there."

"No rush. She's not a problem. Come around back, and I'll let you in."

The phone went dead before she could even thank him. Instead, she called her mom. "I've found her."

"Is she all right?"

"Yeah, she's fine. I'll tell you more when I find out how she ended up where she is."

"Thanks, hon. Again, I'm sorry you got dragged into this."

Moira was, too, but family had to come first. "Go on home, Mom, and relax. I'm not sure how long this will take, so enjoy the quiet while you can."

That her mother didn't argue was telling. "See you soon."

It took less than five minutes to reach the café. The dining area in front was mostly dark, with only a dim light shining through from the kitchen in the back. She'd heard that Titus often worked well past closing time prepping for the next day's meals. Come to think of it, that might explain why he'd left the reception early.

As instructed, she drove around the back of the café. The door opened and Titus stepped outside as soon as she parked the SUV behind a huge motorcycle. "She's doing fine, Officer Fraser. She and Ned have struck up quite the friendship and are enjoying each other's company."

Now that was a surprise. Gram rarely talked to anyone she hadn't known for years. Moira didn't know everyone in town, but she couldn't remember anyone by that name. "Is this Ned new to town?"

Titus looked amused. "That's right. You probably haven't met him. He's a stray who decided to move in with me a few months back. Best guess is he's a German shepherd, golden retriever mix, but don't let Ned's size scare you. He's not the friendliest dog in town, but he has a soft spot for children and childlike souls."

That last category was a surprisingly accurate description of her grandmother these days. "If you don't mind me asking, where did you find Gram? She doesn't usually head in this direction."

"Actually, it was Ned who found her. He pitched a fit and all but dragged me a couple of blocks down toward Fourth Street. Between the two of us, we managed to coax her to come back here with us."

Moira would have loved to have seen that. Gram might be confused, but that didn't mean she couldn't be stubborn as a mule. "How did you know to call me?"

Titus shrugged. "Not many secrets in this town."

True enough. "Well, I'll get her out of your way. Thanks for calling me, Mr. Kondrat. My mom was pretty frantic when she realized Gram was missing."

"Actually, I don't think she's quite ready to leave. She had trouble deciding which flavor of pie she wanted. Right now, she's on her second mini pie and asked for a third." He glanced back inside and then opened the door. "Why don't you come in and have some with her? Maybe a cup of tea, too."

The notion was surprisingly tempting. "I shouldn't. I'm on patrol and could get a call any minute."

But as soon as she stepped inside the café, she knew she wasn't going to rush her grandmother out of there. Gram looked so happy sitting at a small table in the corner, eating pie with one hand while she gently stroked Ned's head with the other.

Without glancing at their host, Moira slowly approached the table and sat down. At least Gram had left home wearing a blouse and slacks instead of her nightgown, like the last time. She was also sporting what had to be one of their host's flannel shirts with the sleeves rolled up several times to accommodate her much shorter arms. Evidently, the dog wasn't the only one with a soft spot for those with childlike souls.

It took a couple of minutes before Gram acknowledged her presence. "I like this dog. Ned looks scary, but he's a marshmallow inside."

"I can see that."

Moira snapped a picture of her grandmother and texted it to her mother, adding a brief note that they'd be home after Gram finished her pie. She'd just hit Send when Titus set a pot of hot water, along with a cup and saucer, in front of her. A second later, he was back with a third mini pie for Gram and a piece of chocolate-cream pie for Moira. Eyeing all that chocolaty goodness, she knew it would take a lot more willpower that she could currently muster to resist the temptation to dig in.

Titus had put a tea bag, two packets of sugar and a lemon wedge on the saucer next to the tea. She picked up the tea bag and stared at the label in confusion. How had he known she liked her tea with two sugars and a squeeze of lemon, or that Earl Grey was her favorite flavor?

"I have other flavors of tea if you don't like Earl Grey."

His deep voice startled her. "No, this is great. It's actually my favorite."

Titus went back to chopping vegetables on a nearby counter. "It's the most popular flavor I carry."

So that explained it. She scooped up a forkful of her pie and closed her eyes in appreciation. "The pie is delicious."

He grunted an acknowledgment of the compliment and kept working. From that point, no one did any talking. Her grandmother happily finished off her last pie while she continued to pet Ned. Other than thanking Titus again for rescuing her grandmother, Moira couldn't think of a single thing to say to the man.

That didn't keep her from wishing she was on the other side of the table, where she could study him without being obvious about it. Gram had an unobstructed view of their host, but seemed totally oblivious to his presence. It was probably better that way. Something told Moira that Titus was the kind of man who was always hyperaware of his surroundings, and the last thing she wanted was for him to pick up on her interest in him. It was strictly professional, of course, but he wouldn't know that. Maybe it was the way he moved that seemed familiar, but she was almost sure they'd never met before she returned to the town.

He wasn't the kind of guy a woman would easily forget.

Moira had some personal experience with that sort of man. Ryan Donovan hadn't been easy to forget, either. They'd met nearly ten years ago, when she'd been fresh out of the academy. Over the course of two months, she'd fallen fast and hard for him. Looking back, she should have known that he was too good to be true. He'd been charming, handsome and sophisticated; she'd had a hard time believing a man like him would be interested in a small-town girl like her. It had taken her way too long to realize that he'd also been careful to avoid letting her snap any pictures of him. That alone should have raised suspicion.

Then came the horrific night Moira had been part of the local backup on a major drug bust, when she'd seen the DEA agents take Ryan into custody along with the rest of his associates. She'd heard a rumor that he'd worked a plea bargain for a reduced sentence. All she knew for sure was that she'd never seen him again nor had she wanted to. It had been ages since she'd thought about Ryan at all, and she was fine with that.

With no photos to refresh her memory, Ryan's image had faded over the ten years since she'd last seen him. The real question was why the man standing behind her had suddenly stirred up those memories. Ryan had been tall like Titus, but not nearly as muscular. His hair had been a much lighter color, and his eyes were blue, not brown. Still, there was an uncanny resemblance between the two men. Was it possible they were related somehow? Cousins, maybe, although Ryan had never mentioned his family that she could remember. Another warning sign she'd missed.

Clearly, the woman she'd been back then hadn't asked enough questions. As a result, the woman she was now would never trust any man so easily again, especially one as deliciously mysterious as Titus Kondrat. Before she could pursue that thought any further, her grandmother spoke up. "I'm tired, Moira."

"Then we'll go home, Gram. Mom will want to hear all about your adventure."

Her grandmother frowned as she looked around at the stainless-steel counters and the hodgepodge of pots and pans hanging from the ceiling on racks. "Why did you bring me here?"

Rather than point out that Gram had found her own way to the café, Moira settled for a white lie. "You had a hankering for some pie."

Gram studied the array of empty ramekins in front of her. "I ate all of those."

It wasn't a question, but Moira answered, anyway. "Mr. Kondrat said you couldn't make up your mind which flavor you wanted, so he served you three of the little ones instead of a great big piece like he gave me. You also wanted to pet Ned there."

Gram looked down at the patient dog and blinked several times as if actually seeing him for the first time. "He's a handsome fellow, isn't he?"

Then she winked at Moira and added, "And so is his dog."

Moira's cheeks flushed hot. "We should be going, Gram. Mr. Kondrat has work to do, and Mom will be concerned."

Gram rolled her eyes. "Your mother is a worrywart, so we shouldn't keep her waiting. The longer I'm gone, the longer her lecture will be. Besides, it's quite a walk back to the house."

Moira wasn't sure which house her grandmother was thinking about, but she was right in both cases. "We don't have to walk, Gram. I have my police cruiser parked right outside."

"Why would you be driving a police car, Moira? Won't they be upset that you borrowed it?"

It was far from the first time Moira had to remind her grandmother about her job and the fact that she was all grown up. "It's my job, Gram, and I'm on duty. I need to get you back home to Mom so I can finish my shift."

To get them both moving in the right direction, she stood up and reached for her wallet. "Mr. Kondrat, how much do I owe you for…?"

One look at their host's face had her putting away her wallet. "Sorry, I meant no insult."

He wiped his hands on a towel and tossed it aside. Then, in a surprising show of gallantry, he offered his arm to her grandmother. "Mrs. Healy, let me escort you to the car."

It was hard not to laugh a little about how her grandmother preened as she set her hand on Titus's outstretched arm. Both dog and man carefully escorted Gram out to the cruiser, waiting patiently for Moira to unlock the doors. Rather than let her diminutive grandmother try to climb up by herself, Titus swept her up in his arms and gently settled her in the passenger seat.

Gram's mind must have cycled back to the present again. Sitting up straighter, she reached out to pat Titus on the cheek. "Thank you for the pie, young man. Please give Ned an extra treat for keeping me company. I didn't mean to be a bother."

"I will, Mrs. Healy, and you weren't any bother at all."

"I'll bring your shirt back." As she spoke, Moira couldn't help but noticed that Titus looked everywhere except directly at her. "And thanks again for everything."

He nodded and stepped back to close the door. Then he and the dog disappeared into the building without a single backward glance. And although she wasn't sure why, Moira found that disappointing.

CHAPTER TWO

TITUS STOOD IN the shadows at the front of his café and watched as the police cruiser slowly turned back onto the main drag through town and disappeared into the night. As its lights faded in the distance, he finally spoke to his silent companion. "Well, dog, that was a close call. Still, it went better than I thought it might."

The unexpected encounter definitely hadn't answered the question he'd been pondering ever since he'd first heard that Moira Fraser had moved back to Dunbar—would she recognize him? The answer appeared to be no, but the odd looks she'd been giving him said that could change at any moment. It had been both a relief and a huge disappointment. "I probably shouldn't be surprised. It's been a lot of years since we last crossed paths."

Besides, he didn't look the same, starting with the fact that he'd packed on a lot of muscle since then. Heck, there were days he didn't recognize his own image in the mirror. His hair was back to its natural dark brown, he no longer wore contacts to alter the color of his eyes and his voice was now rough as sandpaper, thanks to the damage done to his vocal cords during a fight.

Then there were his tattoos. When he'd last seen Moira, he'd only had one or two. Now his forearms were almost entirely etched with ink, the designs all symbols chosen for reasons known only to him. Hidden among the swirls of color were the names of those he'd lost along the way—friends, coworkers, pets and the one woman who had meant far more to him than he'd ever admitted, not just to her but to himself as well.

Ned nudged the side of Titus's leg, a not-so-subtle reminder that he'd wallowed in the disaster of his past long enough. "Fine, fine. I'll get with the program."

By the time Titus reached the kitchen, Ned was already curled up and dozing in his bed. The dog had the right idea, but Titus still had work to do before they could head home for the night. They'd have to walk since he'd taken a long ride on his Harley after leaving

Cade and Shelby's reception early and then driven directly to the café. Ned had shown up only seconds after Titus had parked the bike in the alley, even though he'd left the dog in the house when he'd left for work. He was beginning to regret installing a doggy door so Ned could go in and out as needed. It was only after the door was installed that Titus learned that a six-foot fence was no obstacle if Ned decided he wanted to hang out at the café.

Titus had meant to stay long enough to prep a few things for tomorrow's menu before calling it quits for the day. Instead, Ned had immediately planted himself in front of the back door to the café and herded Titus down the alley and out into the night. As much as Titus had wanted to refuse, the dog wouldn't budge on the issue. As it turned out, Ned had somehow sensed that Mrs. Healy needed rescuing. No matter how many times Titus tried to tell both the dog and himself he was nobody's hero—not anymore—there was no way he would have left the elderly lady out there on the street.

Yeah, he could have called 911 as soon as he'd found her and simply waited until whoever was on duty came to take her home. Instead, he'd loaned Mrs. Healy his shirt to keep her warm and coaxed the shivering woman into following him back to the café, where he could offer her hot tea and all the pie she could eat.

The relief in Moira's voice had been obvious when he'd told her Mrs. Healy was safe and sound in his café. So was the displeasure that he was the one who had found her grandmother. Not much he could do about that. At least now, maybe he didn't have to be so careful about avoiding Moira since she hadn't immediately called him by the name he'd used back in the day. He was no longer that man.

In truth, he never had been. Not really.

Things had gotten a little dicey when he'd screwed up by fixing Moira's tea just the way she liked it. He'd done so out of habit, not realizing his mistake until right after he'd set it down in front of her. She'd noticed, too. It was obvious from the way she stared at the packet of tea and the lemon wedge. What had he been thinking? At least she'd bought his explanation that Earl Grey was the most popular flavor that he carried, which was true.

So was the fact that he carried it because it reminded him of her.

He picked up his knife and went back to work. Slicing and dicing always relaxed him. When he finish chopping the last of the vegetables, he made the pastry he would need for tomorrow's crop of pies and put it in the fridge to rest overnight. It took him another twenty minutes to clean up so the kitchen was ready for Gunner, the short-order cook who handled the early morning rush.

Finally out of anything useful to do, he dried his hands on a towel and tossed it in the hamper in the corner. Satisfied he'd done all he could to get ready for another busy day of feeding the people of Dunbar, he turned off the lights. Ned joined him at the door, ready to walk home.

Before starting out, he rolled the Harley into the shed behind the café and locked the door. His bike probably would have been safe enough out on the street, but there was no use in taking chances. It was a classic 1990 Harley-Davidson Fat Boy that he'd rebuilt himself. The long process had helped him get his head back on straight, and riding it still helped him find peace in moments of high stress.

Once it was secure, he looked around for Ned. The dog was busy sniffing his way up and down the alley, but he came running when Titus gave a sharp whistle. "Let's go home, boy. Tomorrow is another busy day, and I need to get some shut-eye."

Right before they turned down the narrow road that led toward their house, he caught a glimpse of one of the Dunbar police cruisers a few blocks away. There was no telling if it was Moira at the wheel or one of the other officers, not that he cared. He didn't realize that he'd stopped to stare until Ned lunged forward, yanking his leash out of Titus's hand. The dog gave him a disgusted look and then took off running for the house and his bed out on the front porch. No doubt he'd be sound asleep by the time Titus walked the last quarter mile.

"Dog, I don't know why I put up with you."

Which was a lie. Titus still wasn't sure which of them had actually made the decision to become roommates. All he knew was that his house no longer seemed quite so empty, even on the occasional night when Ned opted to sleep outside.

When he finally reached the porch, he stopped to top up Ned's water bowl with the hose. "I'll be turning in soon. If you want in, now's the time."

Ned slowly stood up and stretched. After testing the air one last time, he trotted inside and waited patiently to see where Titus was going to settle. When he headed for the bedroom, Ned jumped up on the couch and staked out the center two cushions, making it clear he wasn't in the mood to share his chosen bed.

Titus circled back to give him a good scratch. "I don't blame you, fella. This might just be one of those nights."

They both knew what he was talking about. Sometimes sleep only came in fits and starts as nightmares from the past kept Titus from getting any real rest. There was no use in both of them having to run on fumes tomorrow. After a quick shower, Titus crawled between cold sheets and stared up at the ceiling, reminding himself it was a good thing that Moira hadn't yet recognized him.

But even if that was true, it still hurt if

she'd forgotten all about him when he'd never been able to get her out of his mind.

"YOU'RE DRESSED FOR work early. I thought your shift didn't start until this afternoon."

Moira finished folding the flannel shirt Titus had loaned her grandmother last night before answering her mother. "I don't have to be at the office until noon, but I have a few errands to run first."

"Is that the shirt Mr. Kondrat loaned Gram last night?"

"Yeah, I told him I would return it."

Her mom leaned against the washer and watched as Moira hung up the rest of the load. "I wish there was something I could do to thank him for helping Gram like he did. Normally I would bake one of my apple pies, but I'm guessing he has all the pie he could ever want."

Moira smiled. "Yeah, that's what I was thinking, too. I thought maybe I'd pick up a nice bottle of wine for him."

"Seriously? I shouldn't stereotype people, but don't you think he looks more like a beer kind of guy?"

Her mother wasn't wrong, but for some

reason Moira thought he might also appreciate a bottle of Malbec. "Well, if he doesn't like drinking wine, he could always cook up something special with it."

Although it would be a criminal waste of such a nice red wine. It was time to change the subject. "How is Gram doing?"

"She's usually pretty connected in the morning. It's only later in the day when things go off the rails."

Moira hung up the last shirt and then gave her mother a hug. "I'm sorry you're having to deal with all of this. Any word from the facility we looked at last week?"

It had been hard for them to finally admit that something had to be done. Her mother had a job with the local school district, but she was running out of leave. Moira's hours changed almost daily depending on what shift she worked. More than that, if she was in the middle of a call, she couldn't simply clock out and rush home at a moment's notice.

It had been one thing to leave Gram alone once she started getting a little forgetful. But now, it wasn't safe to leave her by herself no matter what time of day it was. There was a lady in town who didn't mind staying with

Gram for a few hours if necessary, but Mrs. Redd couldn't do it every day and didn't like to work evenings. That left them no option other than to look for more specialized care. They'd found a local group home close by that they'd liked and were waiting for a room to become available.

"Try to get some rest, Mom. If I can, I'll stop by before I report for duty."

Her mother's smile didn't quite reach her eyes. "I'll be fine, hon. Besides, you have enough on your plate while Chief Peters is gone. Don't spend all your time worrying about us."

Moira nodded as if accepting her marching orders, but they both knew she would still worry about them. That didn't mean that she wouldn't take care of business at work.

"Do you need anything while I'm out and about?"

"Not that I can think of. Elsie Redd said she could stay with Gram while I do the grocery shopping this afternoon. You go ahead and run your errands. I'll put the clean clothes away."

Moira picked up Titus's shirt and kissed her mom on the cheek on her way out of the house. Outside, she stopped to draw in a deep breath of the cool morning air. It had become her ritual. It was a way of setting aside her problems at home before shouldering the ones that came with her job.

Sometimes it even worked.

MOIRA WAS RUNNING out of time if she wanted to deliver Titus's wine and shirt tonight. She could've stopped in the café before she started work or even on her dinner break. Instead, she'd chickened out each time, telling herself that Titus wouldn't want to be bothered while he was working. That was probably true, but it wasn't as if she wanted to show up on the doorstep of his house without warning. He might be busy there, too.

What if he had company? She hadn't heard any rumors that linked Titus's name with a particular woman in town, but that didn't mean he wasn't seeing somebody. Although Moira had a perfectly legitimate reason to show up with his shirt and the wine in hand, it didn't mean his lady friend would appreciate it.

The last time she'd driven past the café, the lights in front were still on, so chances were some members of Titus's staff were hanging around. Deciding to wait a while longer before trying again, she returned to the station to drop off some paperwork. Rather than drive the short distance to the café, she opted to do a quick foot patrol on the way through the small business district in town. She spent too much time in her cruiser as it was, and a little exercise would do her good.

Other than a couple of people out walking with their dogs, there wasn't much going on. That was a good thing, even if it meant she had no excuse to further delay her visit to the café. Sure enough, the lights in front were off this time around. Rather than bang on the front door, she'd go around back like she had on the previous night.

She walked around the side of the building toward the alley in back, but stopped when she heard voices coming from behind the café. She froze, unsure if she should turn back. Rather than make a rash decision, she crept a little farther forward, stopping at the corner of the building to listen. There were two men talking.

"Thanks for making the trip. They seemed in a hurry to get this latest batch."

That gravelly rasp was all too familiar, but who was Titus talking to? And, more importantly, what kind of batch was he talking about?

"Sorry I couldn't get here any earlier, man, but I'll make sure they get the shipment first thing tomorrow."

"Good. Let them know I've reached out to my contacts, and there's already more in the pipeline. When it arrives, I'll call you to set up the distribution."

"Sounds good. Now, I should hit the road."

Moira risked a quick peek around the corner. Unfortunately, the second guy was already closing the rear door of a white van that had definitely seen better days. Without backup close at hand, she couldn't risk getting caught. She retreated half a step to listen in case she could learn more about what they were up to. Luck wasn't with her. All she heard was the sound of a car door opening and closing, followed by the rough rumble of its engine starting.

Luckily, the van continued on down the alley in the other direction. She held her position for another couple of minutes, her mind chock-full of questions with no answers.

Maybe she was overreacting, but all that talk about batches and pipelines and shipments had her flashing back to the drug busts she'd been part of in the past. Too bad she hadn't gotten the license plate on the van so she could run it when she got back to the station. The guy had been standing right in front of it when she peeked around the corner, and now it was too late. Even if she could still see the van, it would be too far away to make out the numbers and letters.

Maybe she needed to keep a closer eye on what went on behind the café at night. It seemed Titus had other reasons to hang around after closing time, ones that had nothing to do with chopping onions and carrots.

Taking a deep breath, and hoping she looked calmer than she felt, she started forward only to let out a shriek when she ran right into Titus as soon as she turned the corner. He reached out to steady her before stepping back. He crossed his arms over his chest and stared down at her with his mouth quirked up in a small smile as if he found the situation amusing.

"Tell me, Officer Fraser, did you hear anything interesting while sneaking around and listening in on a private conversation?"

He might think this was funny, but she didn't. "I heard enough to wonder what else you might be selling these days besides chocolate-cream pie."

He flinched just enough to signal she'd scored a direct hit. "Feel free to wonder all you want. Now, if you'll excuse me, I need to lock up and head home."

The smart thing would be to walk away, but instead of going into full retreat, she marched up to the door and let herself in. Titus was expecting her, because he was leaning against the counter with his legs crossed at the ankle and looking far more relaxed than he had been a few seconds before. Obviously trying to put her off balance, he gave her a long look, starting at her head and wandering southward, then back up again, his gaze snagging briefly on the gift bag in her hand.

"Look, Moira, I don't know what you're doing here, and I don't care. Right now, I'm tired and just want to go home. Whatever you want will have to wait." He turned his back to her and began wiping down the counter.

"I didn't come here to spy on you."

He sighed and tossed the rag he'd been using into the sink. "Then why are you here? If it's for more of the chocolate pie, I'll send some home with you if that will get you out from underfoot faster."

The pie sounded good, but she didn't want to be any further in debt to him than she already was. "Actually, I came to give you this."

When she held out the bag, he stared at it as if she was trying to hand him a live snake. "What's that?"

Since he showed no inclination to take it from her, she stepped close enough to set it on the counter. "Your shirt and a thank-you gift for helping my grandmother."

"You shouldn't have."

Considering how uncomfortable Titus looked at the moment, he probably meant that. Too bad. "Ordinarily Mom would've baked you a pie, but she figured you already had enough of those. She thought you were probably more of a beer guy, but I decided to buy you a bottle of wine instead."

When he remained frozen right where he stood, she pulled the bottle out of the bag and forced him to take it from her hand. He held the wine out at arm's length and frowned at the label as if it would give him cooties.

"If you don't like what I picked out, feel free to regift it. I'm sure you know someone who would like a nice Malbec from Argentina."

He swallowed hard and then nodded. "It's a surprising choice for a small-town girl, but I won't be regifting this. It's one of my favorite wines. I might wait for a special occasion, but I will enjoy it."

Okay, then. The crisis had passed, although she couldn't imagine why this suddenly felt like a pivotal moment in their relationship. Not that they had one. When he gently set the bottle back in the bag after wrapping it in his clean shirt, she took that as a signal it was time to leave.

She made a show of checking her watch before opening the door. "Well, I should get back to the office. TJ is due to relieve me in half an hour."

Titus must have hustled locking up because he caught up with her before she reached the corner. He matched his stride to hers as they walked along the side of the building. "I didn't hear your cruiser when you arrived."

Moira pointed out the obvious. "That's because I walked."

"Well, that explains it."

She glanced up at him. "Explains what?"

"How you got so close without me noticing."

Rather than get tangled up in that whole situation again, she kept it light and gave him a superior look. "Sir, I'll have you know I am a highly trained police officer. How we do what we do is a trade secret."

That he laughed a little pleased her more than it should have. She had another question of her own. "But if you didn't hear me coming, why were you waiting for me when I came around the corner?"

Her imagination was probably working overtime, but for a second there was something oddly familiar about his expression before he finally answered her question. "Café owners have secrets, too."

Then he walked away into the darkness, leaving her staring at his back.

CHAPTER THREE

IT TOOK TITUS longer than normal to get home, mainly because he'd stood watch until Moira made it back inside the station. She'd kick his backside if she found out he was looking out for her. He also knew that she was perfectly capable of defending herself, but he'd sleep better knowing that she'd made it to the end of her shift safely.

That didn't mean he wasn't still a little bit ticked off that she'd decided to spy on him and Ryder out in the alley. Instead of simply asking what they were up to, she'd immediately leaped to the conclusion that he was dealing drugs out of the back of his café. Yeah, she didn't know this iteration of him well enough to know any better. That didn't mean he appreciated her lack of faith in him. Logic didn't enter into the equation.

He could've settled the problem by admitting it had been a shipment of donated dog food and cat litter for a group of animal shelters in the area. Any one of the shelter managers would vouch for him if Moira wanted to verify he was telling her the truth. But, stubborn man that he was, he wanted her to simply trust him. Stupid, but he'd never been smart when it came to her.

Heaven knew he should've walked away from her the minute he realized she was going to be more than a passing interest for him. That mistake had caused them both a lot of pain. If…no, *when* she figured out that he and Ryan Donovan were one and the same, she'd likely gut him with a dull spoon. Or, worse yet, rat him out to the rest of the town by exposing the fact that their favorite chef had been arrested in a major drug bust a decade ago.

Ned was waiting for him on the front porch. "Sorry I'm late. Stuff happened."

The dog didn't want excuses. He only cared about the delay in getting his kibble delivered on time. As soon as Titus opened the front door, Ned shoved past him to stand over his food dish, his displeasure clear.

"Fine, fine. I'll feed you as soon as I set this bag down."

He unwrapped the bottle of wine and set both it and his clean shirt on the counter. After filling Ned's dish, he cut up a leftover hamburger and added a few pieces to the mix. He knew he was spoiling the dog, but a man had to take care of his friends. Ned gave the bowl a good sniff and acknowledged Titus's efforts with a slow wag of his tail.

With his roommate taken care of, Titus popped the top on one of the microbrews that Max Volkov had given him a week or so ago. After taking a long swig, he smiled. Moira's mother wasn't wrong. He drank far more beer than he did wine. A cold brew really hit the spot after a long day at work or while sitting out on Cade's porch sharing pizza.

Wine was more of a special-occasion beverage as far as he was concerned, especially a pricey bottle of imported Malbec. It was the kind of wine a man bought for the special woman in his life, which was why he'd only served that particular vintage once. Just staring at the label was stirring up all kinds of memories, ones he tried not to think about very often.

Knowing he'd missed his chance at having a real life with the one woman he'd ever loved hurt too much.

An argument could be made that he'd been a fool to settle in Dunbar. There were other small towns and other run-down cafés that he could've bought. But when he'd finally broken free from the chains of his past, he hadn't even considered any other option than the one he'd chosen. It was probably a sign that, despite his best efforts, he hadn't quite given up his love of adrenaline rushes and taking risks.

He'd chosen Dunbar for one reason and one reason only. It was Moira Fraser's hometown. She hadn't been living here when he'd signed the paperwork on the café, but he'd known there was always a good chance that she might move back. If nothing else, she had family in Dunbar and would come back periodically to visit them. Add in that his was the only eatery in town other than a take-out pizza joint and a tavern, their paths were bound to cross again at some point.

So far, it was obvious that Moira hadn't consciously recognized Titus. He could probably thank the damage done to his voice and face ten years ago for that. Regardless, her subconscious was clearly hard at work. Otherwise, of all the possible choices in fine wines, why had she bought him a bottle of the same kind they'd enjoyed with the only dinner he had ever cooked for her?

Rather than torture himself by adding the Malbec to the small wine rack sitting on the back corner of his kitchen counter, he tucked it away over the refrigerator in the small cabinet that he hardly ever opened. Out of sight and out of mind. Yeah, like that ever worked.

He finished off his beer and tossed the bottle in the recycling bin. "I'm going to bed, dog. Keep the racket down so I can get some sleep."

Rather than curling up on the sofa, Ned followed him into the bedroom and hopped up on the bed. Titus glared at him. "Fine, you can sleep in here if you want, but pick a side of the bed and stay there. No hogging the middle."

When Titus stepped back out of the bathroom, all he could do was stop and stare. Ned had expressed his opinion on the subject by stretching out across both pillows at the top of the bed. Titus finally laughed. "Good one, Ned. Now move."

Satisfied that his effort to yank Titus's chain had been a success, Ned shifted to the far side of the bed and fell back to sleep within seconds. Still chuckling, Titus made himself comfortable and did the same.

WITH EVERYTHING THAT was going on, Moira felt a little guilty stealing time out of her day for purely selfish reasons. Her mom had taken Gram to a doctor appointment, so there wasn't anything she needed to be doing at home. Besides, she didn't have to report into the office until midafternoon. Finally, she reminded herself that even her boss had been known to sneak in a lunch date with his fiancée now and then. An hour to kick back and share a few laughs with a friend would do her some good.

The only drawback was where she and Carli were meeting for lunch—Titus's café. Short of driving to another town, there was no other choice. Besides, Carli would likely ask a lot of uncomfortable questions as to why Moira would want to do that. She didn't want to explain that it had been two days since she and Titus had last crossed paths, and she wasn't particularly excited about the possibility of doing so again.

How was she supposed to act around a man she'd pretty much accused of engaging in criminal activity in the alley behind his café? Looking back, she couldn't blame him for being a little ticked off about it, but she hadn't been wrong to wonder why they'd been tossing around words like *supplier*, *batch* and *pipeline*. It would be one thing if Titus had simply explained what they had been doing, but he hadn't. He'd even gone so far as to tell her that he had secrets.

No surprise there.

The door to the café opened, and Carli poked her head out. "Well, are you coming in or not?"

Was it too late to claim she'd been called into work early? It was tempting, but then she spotted the man himself standing not far behind Carli, smirking just enough to set Moira's teeth on edge. "I'm coming in."

As usual, the place was pretty much packed, but Titus led them to a table near the back that had just been cleared. He handed them menus, greeting Carli by name. His dark eyes briefly met Moira's gaze. "It's been a while, Officer Fraser."

As she stalked past him, she muttered, "Not long enough."

He kept pace with her, then leaned in close and whispered, "If I'd known you were coming, I would've made sure to have the chocolate pie on the menu."

The rough rumble of his voice sent a shiver straight through the heart of her, causing her to almost stumble. Luckily, she caught herself before anyone noticed. Well, anyone other than Titus himself. She was pretty sure he was laughing as he turned away to greet another customer.

Carli knew Moira liked to keep an eye on her surroundings and preferred to sit with her back to the wall, so she automatically took the other seat. There was no way Moira could ask her to switch places without raising yet another bunch of questions. Her friend knew her too well.

She and Carli had gone to school together and stayed in touch over the years. Whenever Moira had come home for a visit, they got together to catch up on each other's lives. At least once a year, Carli would come stay with

Moira for a few days. Sometimes they took in a traveling Broadway show or else treated themselves to hours in the spa at one of the local casino hotels. They'd even gone camping a time or two.

The best part was if either of them was going through a rough patch, the other one came running with a bottle of wine and a shoulder to cry on. Carli had been there for Moira ten years ago when her love life had imploded, and Moira had reciprocated when her friend had gone through an unexpected and unwanted divorce.

The bottom line was that Moira was sitting across from the one person who could read her like a book. She'd have to watch every word she said and every move she made. The last thing she needed was for her friend to pick up on Moira's intense awareness of the man weaving his way through the café as he handed out menus to newcomers and glanced in her direction whenever he thought she might not notice.

"So how are things going with Chief Peters gone?"

Carli's question snapped Moira's attention back to her where it should be. "Quiet for the most part. The city council decided I need to give them daily reports to make sure I'm staying on top of things. Cade won't appreciate them poking their noses in department business, and it's a huge waste of time."

Her smile turned a bit wicked. "I make everything as dry as possible. Nothing like statistics and bar graphs to bore the socks off people."

Carli chuckled. "Serves them right."

Their server put in an appearance. She set a glass of water in front of Carli and a pot of tea in front of Moira—Earl Grey with lemon and two sugars. After she took their orders and left, Carli gave Moira a puzzled look. "Do you come in here so often that they already know how you like your tea?"

"No, actually I don't. It must have been a lucky guess."

Her friend studied her for several seconds. "That's pretty specific for a lucky guess."

The man was definitely messing with her. "Maybe that's how they serve it to everybody."

Still looking dubious, Carli glanced back over her shoulder toward the kitchen and then back at Moira. "I order tea sometimes. I always get a bowl with half a dozen different flavors of tea bags in it and no lemon unless I ask for it."

Then she pointed at the small container on the table that was stuffed full of sugar and sweetener packets. "Did Titus think there weren't enough of those on the table for one cup of tea?"

Before Moira could come up with any kind of explanation that wasn't completely ridiculous, Titus came back with their orders himself. After serving Carli, he set Moira's bacon-burger platter on the table. It was piled high with at least double the normal amount of sweet-potato fries and came with two bowls of dipping sauces. One was tartar sauce and the other was ranch dressing. Carli's eyes almost bugged out of her head, but at least she didn't say a word.

"Can I get anything else for you two ladies?"

Not trusting herself to be civil, Moira kept her eyes on her food and shook her head. Carli managed to be a little more polite. "We're good, Mr. Kondrat."

"Let me know if that changes."

As he walked away, Moira stuffed three

fries into her mouth at once to avoid having to answer the litany of questions that Carli was bound to ask. The ruse failed miserably. As soon as she swallowed, her friend pounced. "Okay, what's up between you and Dunbar's mystery man? And don't tell me nothing is going on. I eat here at least once a week, and I've never seen him act like this."

"Like what?"

Her friend held up her fingers to count off the facts. "He seated us himself. He usually just points and tells people where to sit. He sent tea to the table just the way you like it, and he delivered our food personally."

She stopped to point at Moira's plate. "That's enough sweet-potato fries for two people, so he knows you like them. You didn't ask for any special dipping sauces, but he brought your two favorites. Shall I continue?"

Even Moira had to admit Carli's evidence was pretty compelling. "Did anyone ever suggest you should've been a prosecuting attorney? After that list, any jury in the country would vote to convict."

Her friend leaned forward, elbows on the table. "Which raises the question of what you two might be guilty of. I won't be happy if you've been holding out on me."

Better to go with the safe part of the truth and hope that was enough to satisfy Carli's curiosity. "For starters, the only times I've eaten here, he's been working in back. However, Gram got out again the other night, and Mr. Kondrat found her. He brought her back here and served her pie and tea while he waited for me to come pick her up. When I arrived, she wasn't quite done with her treats, so he offered me tea and pie, too."

"And?"

"And what? Isn't that enough?"

Her friend's expression turned more sympathetic. "I'm so sorry about Gram, and it was nice of him to come to the rescue. Having said that, I get that might be why he knows how you like your tea, but it doesn't explain the fries, the dipping sauces or the way you avoided looking him in the eye when he was standing right there. I've never seen you act so skittish before."

Moira set her burger back on her plate. It was tempting to rail at her friend, but this wasn't Carli's problem. It was Moira's, plain and simple. She sighed as she dipped a fry in the ranch dressing. "I'm not afraid of Titus. There's just something about him that sets my teeth on edge. It's a cop thing, not a woman-versus-man thing. I've put a lot of men who look like him behind bars over the years."

That clearly shocked Carli. "But he's friends with Chief Peters."

"I know." She ate the fry and reached for another one. Talking about what it was like to be a cop with a civilian was never easy, even if the other person was a good friend. "You know me. I've never seen a puzzle I didn't want to solve, and that man is definitely a puzzle. No one knows where he came from or what he did before he moved to Dunbar. Heck, even Bea hasn't been able to figure it out, and you know all gossip flows through her bakery."

A shadow fell across the table, startling them both. She wasn't the only one relieved to see it was Rita, one of the two sisters who worked the day shift at the café. She had two pieces of pie in her hands, both of them chocolate-cream. She smiled at Moira. "It's your lucky day. It turns out we had exactly two pieces of your favorite pie left. Titus said it's on the house since he'd told you it wasn't on the menu today."

Moira unclenched her teeth long enough to be polite. "Thanks, Rita. Tell Mr. Kondrat we appreciate his generosity."

"Will do."

Carli waited until Rita disappeared back into the kitchen before speaking. "I don't remember the subject of pie coming up earlier when we gave her our orders."

"It didn't."

Knowing two words wouldn't satisfy Carli's curiosity, Moira surrendered to the inevitable. "Titus gave me chocolate-cream pie when I was here with Gram. It was delicious, and he must have noticed how much I liked it. When he walked us to the table, he quietly mentioned that if he'd known I was coming in, he would've made sure there was chocolate-cream pie on the menu."

"Interesting." Her friend's eyes were alight with amusement when she added, "I assume you've noticed that he's an attractive man."

Seriously? "If you think he's all that, why don't you make him a casserole?"

Carli slapped her hand onto her forehead.

"Gee, now why didn't I think of that? Especially when it worked so well last time."

Wow, there was a lot of sarcasm packed into that statement. Carli had been one of the women who had tried to catch Cade Peters's eye when he'd first moved to town by providing him with a whole lot of home-cooked meals. There had definitely been some sour grapes when he'd chosen Shelby Michaels instead, especially considering she hadn't baked a single casserole for him.

Moira smirked just a little. "I'm just saying."

"Okay, I'll tell you why. First, it obviously didn't work the last time. Second, Titus is a better cook than I could ever hope to be. Anything I baked for him would only be a big disappointment and would probably end up as a free meal for that huge dog that hangs around in the kitchen back there."

It was hard to argue with her logic. Besides, Moira wouldn't want to see her friend get hurt again. The meltdown of Carli's marriage had left wounds on her friend's heart that had only started to heal, and she needed a man who would treat her gently. Having seen the way Titus had been with her grandmother, she knew he was capable of toning down his intensity if the situation called for it. But that wasn't who Titus was at the core. She was convinced of that much.

Moira noticed two men, both members of the city council, headed for the door, and she stifled the urge to groan when they suddenly detoured in her direction. "Mr. Hayes, Mr. Crisp."

Julius Hayes checked his watch. "Officer Fraser, do you really have time to be socializing in the middle of the day when you're supposed to be in charge of the police department? I've heard that there have been reports of two incidents of theft over the past two days. Something about pet supplies missing from the feedstore and the market."

"I know about the thefts, Mr. Hayes. We wrote up reports and took statements from the two businesses. No one knows when the items were actually taken, only that their inventory of canned cat and dog food was off by several items. Neither business has security cameras, and no one saw anything. That doesn't leave us much to investigate, but we'll be checking back with the owners periodically to see if it happens again. Oscar is on duty and knows he can call me for assistance if need be. Since I'm on duty tonight, I'm not scheduled to report in for another hour."

Herb Crisp wasn't having it. "As the acting chief, you should be—"

Another unwelcome party joined the discussion, cutting off whatever the man was about to say with a simple look. He stared at them. "Gentlemen, since you've finished your two-hour lunch, I suggest you pay your bills and leave."

As entertaining as it was to see the two councillors bolt toward the cash register, Moira didn't appreciate Titus poking his nose in her business. "I was dealing with the situation. You didn't have to do that."

"Yeah, I did. I don't put up with anyone hassling my customers no matter who they are." He walked away without giving Moira a chance to respond.

Carli waited until Titus reached the two councillors to ring up their checks before speaking. "Wow, that was intense. I bet those two will never do that again."

"Maybe not, but I don't want or need Titus butting his nose in my business. If he does it again, we'll be having words." Because she didn't need him making her look as if she needed a big, strong man to run interference for her, especially in front of the two councillors who had questioned Cade's decision to leave her in charge.

"We'd better get the pie boxed up to go while we finish off our burgers. I really should report in."

Carli finished cutting her burger in half to make it easier to manage and then pointed her knife in Moira's direction. "Fine, but just know I can't remember the last time I've seen you this worked up about a man. You might not realize it, but you can't seem to tear your eyes off Titus even when you're mad at him."

Moira realized it, all right. Try as she could to convince herself it was all because of what had gone on in the alley the other night, that story didn't hold water. No, there was just something about the way that man moved that drew her gaze every time he wandered through the diner. There was such power in those broad shoulders and lean muscles. And silly as it was, she'd always had a thing for men with their sleeves rolled up to reveal powerful forearms. She would have never thought she'd find that many tattoos attractive, but she'd really like to study his artwork up close.

Carli snickered. "There you go doing it again."

Having a fair complexion made it impossible to hide the fact that she was blushing. "Enough, Carli. Please."

"Okay, I'll lay off for now. Just know we'll be revisiting this conversation at another time."

Surrendering to the inevitable, Moira shrugged. "That's what I figured."

Hopefully she'd have better answers for her friend about this odd compulsion when the time came. Sadly, she wouldn't bet on that happening.

CHAPTER FOUR

TEN MINUTES AFTER Moira went on duty, her day took a definite turn for the weird. Oscar had ducked his head in the door long enough to say that two people had shown up at the front desk wanting to report a major crime. He'd been about to relieve TJ out on patrol, so Moira told him to escort the pair to the conference room and tell them she'd join them shortly.

She closed out the file she'd been updating and picked up her clipboard that held blank report forms. Oscar hadn't mentioned any names, but she recognized both people. A widow in her early seventies, Mrs. Zimmer shared a duplex with her cousin about two blocks away from where Moira lived. Edward Sandis had a small house in the same neighborhood. He'd retired from the forestry department a few weeks back.

Considering they had both reported their

pets missing within the last few days, it wasn't surprising when they each pulled out a flyer that featured Mrs. Zimmer's calico cat and Mr. Sandis's long-haired dachshund. Assuming they were there for a status update on the department's efforts to locate the missing animals, Moira set her clipboard on the table. "I'm sorry, but there hasn't been progress. We've all been keeping an eye out for Bitsy and Clyde. I've also checked in with a couple of the closest animal shelters to see if they've picked up any strays that fit their descriptions."

Mr. Sandis waved off her apology. "We know you've done your best, Officer Fraser. That's not why we're here. We wanted to update you on what's happened since we first reported the problem. I learned that her cat was missing when our paths crossed when I was posting my flyers. In fact, they disappeared within an hour of each other. Needless to say, we've both been doing everything we can to find both of our pets."

He smiled at the older woman. "We've each cruised different parts of town looking for Bitsy and Clyde with no luck. Until yesterday, that is."

Then he pointed at two plastic bags sitting in front of him on the table. From where Moira was sitting, it looked as if they each held what looked like a typewritten note and a legal-size envelope. After sliding them across the table toward Moira, Mr. Sandis said, "We've had a break in the case. The two of us found these letters in our mailboxes yesterday afternoon. We put them in the bags like they do on television to protect the forensic evidence. Thought you might want to dust them for fingerprints or something."

Moira didn't want to rain on their parade, but that wasn't going to happen. Small police departments like theirs didn't have their own labs. Instead, they depended on the county sheriff's department for any forensic investigations. It was doubtful—if not laughable—that the sheriff would waste limited resources on a missing pets.

That didn't mean Moira wouldn't give it her best effort to figure out what was going on. Picking up the bags, she quickly scanned the notes. The messages were identical:

If you want your pet back, put $20.00 in the enclosed sandwich bag and leave it in the old phone booth behind the abandoned gas station.

"Seriously? You think someone is actually holding your pets ransom? For twenty dollars?"

It was hard not to groan when both people immediately nodded. By that point, Mrs. Zimmer was smiling big-time. "Yes, that's exactly what happened."

Moira tried to get her head around the idea. "It seems more likely to me that someone saw your flyers and decided to see if you'd pay up on the off chance it would get your pets back."

"But that's just it. We did put the money in the old phone booth. When I woke up this morning, Bitsy was back home."

It had to be a coincidence. "Did she look like she'd been living on the street for a few days? Was she starving?"

Mr. Sandis picked up the conversation. "No, actually, I'd have to say that wherever Clyde has been, he was well treated. His nails were clipped, he'd had a bath and his coat had been brushed. He hasn't looked that good since the last time my wife took him to that fancy dog groomer in Seattle."

"The same with my cat. I don't know what brand of pet shampoo the kidnapper used, but Bitsy's fur was so soft and smooth. Smelled good, too."

Moira was happy for them, but she wasn't sure what they wanted her to do now. "I'm glad it's all turned out for the best. However, I'm pretty sure the sheriff's office won't have time to process the evidence, especially since the pets have come home."

Mrs. Zimmer looked disappointed by Moira's assessment of the situation, but Mr. Sandis didn't look surprised. "I thought that might be the case. But all things considered, I thought it was worth a shot."

"What things?"

He brought up a picture on his cell phone and passed it over. "When I went to take down the flyers on Clyde and Bitsy, I saw these."

The picture was a close-up of three more flyers about missing pets—two small dogs and another cat. All of them were from the same general area where Mr. Sandis and Mrs. Zimmer lived.

"I hadn't heard about these. I'll have to check with Oscar and TJ to see if either of them have taken reports about more missing animals. Is it okay if I forward these pictures to myself? I'd like to reach out to the owners to see what I can learn."

"Sure thing. Do you want to keep the ransom notes, too?"

She reached for her clipboard and began to fill out the form. "Yes, I need to log them in as evidence."

That had both of her guests sitting up straighter in their chairs. This was probably the closest either of them had ever come to being part of an official police investigation. If she was a betting woman, either or both of them would head straight for the bakeshop down the street to announce the news. It was tempting to ask them to keep the information to themselves for the time being, but she decided that it probably wasn't possible to keep a lid on the situation for long, anyway. Besides, there was no telling how many people they'd already talked to before deciding to bring the ransom notes to the police department.

It didn't take long to finish the report. She

wrote the case number on the back of her business card for each of them and then stood. "Thanks for bringing this to our attention. I'll reach out to the other pet owners to make sure they know to contact our office if they get a note like this or if their pet comes home."

"That's great." Mr. Sandis held out his hand. "Thanks for taking this seriously, Officer Fraser. I know compared to the cases you probably handled in Seattle, a lost cat or dog may not seem all that important. But if you'd heard my wife crying when we thought we'd lost Clyde forever, you'd know how much it meant to us."

"I understand, Mr. Sandis. Please tell your wife that I'm so pleased that Clyde is back home where he belongs."

She walked with them to the front door of the station. He was right, of course. It was highly unlikely that her former department would have paid much attention to this kind of case. It was a prime example of how police work in a small town was understandably different from working in a major city. She might have some regrets about walking away from her job in Seattle, but that didn't mean she wasn't going to do her best to serve the people of Dunbar.

As she returned to her desk, she pondered the case. What kind of person kidnapped a cat and then asked for such a paltry ransom amount? Especially when it sounded like they'd spent a fair amount of money on grooming products and pet food, returning the animal well-fed and shampooed. Well, unless the kidnappings tied in with the stolen pet supplies.

It was a puzzle all right. Shaking her head, she went back to reading the report she'd been working on when Oscar had interrupted her. Once that was finished, she'd start making some phone calls.

THE FIRST HOUR Moira was on patrol was blissfully quiet. Unfortunately, a call from Dispatch changed that. "Tell Shay Barnaby I should be there in less than five minutes."

Moira hung up the call and picked up speed. A few blocks later, she spotted the commotion that had been reported to Dispatch. Evidently, some truckers had gotten rowdy enough at Barnaby's tavern that Shay himself had escorted them out of his fine establishment. Considering his reputation, he'd probably used his boot to hurry them on out the door. She wasn't taking the situation lightly, but she would've liked to have seen that for herself. In his midthirties, Barnaby was a former Recon Marine, and no one with a lick of sense would take him on when he got riled up.

He understood the nature of his clientele and on the whole was pretty tolerant of their behavior. If he couldn't handle the kind of crew that routinely hung out in the tavern, he had definitely picked the wrong line of work. From what Moira had heard, only one thing would result in him tossing out paying customers: someone had said or done something to offend one of his employees. Moira actually respected the man for being so highly protective of his staff. This time a trucker had gotten a bit handsy with one of the servers, a definite no-no. When the guy's two drunken buddies had laughed, Barnaby had ordered all three of them to vacate the premises pronto.

The trio had made the mistake of thinking they stood a chance against Shay Barnaby. He had them out the door and back on the street before they knew what hit them. In the process, he'd also confiscated their keys to make sure none of them got behind the wheel until they sobered up. That was smart of him, even if it left the three wandering around on the street with nowhere to go and no way to get there even if they did.

Hence the call to Moira. Left to their own devices, there was no telling what kind of trouble they would get into. She parked her cruiser and got out, but not until she put in a call to the county sheriff's department to let them know she would likely need an assist.

She walked toward where the trucker and his friends were wandering around, peering in shop windows as if on the hunt for another watering hole. As soon as one of them spotted her headed their way, they stood shoulder-to-shoulder and watched her approach. When they stepped off the sidewalk into the glow of a nearby streetlight, she recognized the guy on the left. Jimmy Hudson had been a year ahead of her in school, and his mother still lived about a block from her mom's house.

"Jimmy, looks like you might need to call someone to come get you. If you don't have your phone handy, I can make the calls for you."

He squinted in her direction. "Do I know you?"

"I'm Moira Fraser. We went to school together." She tapped the badge on her uniform shirt. "Actually, it's Officer Fraser now. Do you still live with your mom?"

He snorted with laughter and jerked his thumb toward the guys standing next to him. "No, I live with them."

Then he gave her what he probably thought was a sexy leer and waggled his eyebrows. "As you can see, I'm all grown up. Maybe you should come home with us."

Praying for patience, Moira tried a different tack. "Do you live within walking distance or do I need to call someone to come pick you up?"

Jimmy puffed out his chest and widened his stance. "Doesn't matter. I parked my truck out back. I can drive myself home as soon as you arrest that Barnaby guy for stealing my keys."

He waved his hand in the general direction of his two companions. "Theirs, too. He had no right to do that. We didn't do anything wrong."

"That's not what I heard. According to Mr.

Barnaby, he asked you to leave because you disrespected at least one member of his staff. You know he doesn't put up with that kind of stuff. He also doesn't let people drive who've had too much to drink."

"I apologized to her." Jimmy frowned and added, "At least I meant to. He tossed us out before I had a chance. When you go inside to get our keys, you tell him that it's all his fault."

Like that was going to happen. "First things first. We need to get the three of you home. Then I'll talk to Barnaby about your keys. You can pick them up at the station tomorrow, provided you cooperate and go home quietly."

When Jimmy turned his back to her to confer with his buddies, she knew they weren't going be smart about this. It was time to check on those reinforcements from the county. The trouble was that the county deputies were likely out on their own calls.

While the three men were distracted, she checked back to find out how much longer it would be until help arrived. Hearing the best-case scenario was an ETA of fifteen to twenty minutes, she quickly dialed TJ's number. He answered on the second ring, sounding blissfully alert despite the late hour. He was out his front door and running for his car before she finished explaining. She only needed to keep a lid on things long enough for him to get there.

Jimmy abruptly turned back around, an ugly smile on his face. "We don't want to go home. We want to go back inside. Barnaby can't refuse to serve us because of a little misunderstanding with that waitress. He never asked for our side of the story."

That was probably because Barnaby had seen it play out in real time, but pointing that out wasn't going to help the situation. Moira offered the best deal she could. "Jimmy, for the last time, the three of you need to go home and sleep it off. Otherwise you're going to end up behind bars, and it won't be here in Dunbar. You'll be the guests of the county, and none of us want that to happen."

He made a show of looking up and down the street. "Funny, I don't see any county deputies anywhere around here. It's just us and one lady cop all by her lonesome."

When he took several steps in her direction, Moira stood her ground. "You don't want to do this, Jimmy. What will your mama say?"

"Don't know. Don't care."

He kept coming. "Like I said, you've got no backup. Chief Peters is out of town on his honeymoon. That old cop, Oscar something, he wouldn't be much help even if he was here."

Jimmy wasn't wrong, but Moira wasn't going to admit that in front of a civilian. "Who can I call for you?"

One of the others finally chimed in. "Like he said. We don't need no calls made. Make Barnaby give our keys back or things are gonna get rough."

Moira wasn't the only one who jumped when Titus prowled out of the shadows from across the street with that huge dog at his side. He was on Moira's left, a few steps behind her, as if making it clear that he was there as backup, not trying to take charge of the situation. That didn't keep him from injecting himself into the conversation.

"What was that you said, Toby? Because it sure sounded like you were threatening Officer Fraser."

The cold fury threaded through his words had all three men taking a step back, even as it had Moira's temper flashing hot. She had the situation under control with additional support on the way. But now wasn't the time for that discussion; that would come later, when the current problem had been dealt with. The guy Titus had called Toby swallowed hard and held up his hands as if hoping to placate the furious man standing beside her.

"Sorry, Titus. I didn't mean nothing. We were just messing with her. We didn't know she was yours."

Moira cringed. *Great.* The last thing she needed was for rumors linking her name to Titus's to start circulating in town, especially if the city council caught wind of him backing her up on a call. They already doubted her ability to do her job. Before she could set Toby straight, Titus did it for her.

"Officer Fraser is her own woman, knucklehead. But from what I heard from Shay Barnaby, Officer Fraser is not the first woman you nitwits insulted tonight. I won't stand for it and neither will Barnaby. You're all banned from my café and his tavern until further notice."

Well, wasn't that just dandy. Nothing like throwing gas on the fire. He had to know that kind of threat wasn't going to help the situation. She glared at him and then at Toby. "Like he said, I speak for myself. Here's how this is going to play out. Settle down now and I'll make sure you get home. We'll return your keys in the morning. The other option is spending the night behind bars. It's your choice."

Toby had sobered up enough to realize how much trouble they were in, but Jimmy was still going full steam ahead. "I ain't afraid of either of you. Besides, it's still three against two."

Titus's dog barked and flashed his teeth, maybe to point out that the odds were actually even. She didn't know about Jimmy, but she wouldn't want to face off against Ned… or his owner, for that matter.

"Not three, Jimmy. I'm out of this." Toby stumbled back a few steps, holding up his hands. His bloodshot eyes pleaded with Moira to believe he no longer wanted to be part of this disaster. If he actually meant it, it would help even up the odds.

She pointed toward the sidewalk behind him. "Toby, go sit down on the curb. Officer

Shaw will be along any second. He'll drive you home when we're done here."

Toby immediately backpedaled over to the curb and sat down. The as-yet-unnamed third member of the group looked at Jimmy, her and then Titus. "Is that offer good for me, too?"

When she nodded, he joined Toby on the curb, putting several feet between them. Both men were smart enough to keep their hands in plain sight and didn't move an inch. Rather than follow their lead, Jimmy made a break for it, making a quick turn to charge back toward the tavern.

He might have been a football star in high school, but his glory days were long gone. Moira caught up with him before he'd gone ten feet. Using his own momentum against him, she had him on the ground and cuffed before he knew what hit him. He tried to roll over, but she held him in position. That didn't mean she wasn't relieved to see TJ finally arrive. He parked his car and came running.

"What can I do?"

"Let's get him into the back of my cruiser. The county deputy is on his way. He can take him to the county lockup."

She nodded in the direction of the other two. "They made smarter decisions. I told them you'd see they got home. I'll pick up their keys from Shay Barnaby after we're done here. They can get them back in the morning."

They dragged Jimmy up to his feet. "This one will get his back when and if the judge says he can."

When they'd tucked Jimmy into the back seat of her vehicle, TJ frowned. "Sorry you had to do this all by yourself."

She hadn't, not really. But when she looked around for Titus, he had disappeared as quickly as he had appeared. She fully intended to rip into him but good for showing up unwanted and uninvited, but that discussion would be private. His intentions had been good—it just wasn't his job.

It was hers.

TITUS STARED UP at the stars overhead as he replayed the confrontation in front of Barnaby's in his head. Looking back, it was obvious that Moira had already called for backup before he had charged into the situation. There wasn't a doubt in his mind that the woman would come looking for him sometime soon.

"Darn it, dog, I screwed up big-time."

Ned didn't care. He was too busy sniffing around the bushes along the front edge of their yard. He took it personally if another dog or any other critter decided to make a pit stop in his territory. He stopped at one bush long enough to grumble a bit before lifting his leg. His job done, he trotted to the porch and waited for Titus to catch up.

As he unlocked the door, he couldn't help but admire the way Moira had faced off against the three fools without backing down an inch. She'd given them every possible chance to make a smart decision. It had even worked two times out of three. Chalk that up as a win for the good guys. Too bad Jimmy hadn't made the same decision.

None of them would be happy about being banned from the café and Shay's place for any length of time, but it served them right.

He flipped on the lights and headed into the kitchen. Ned followed along in case Titus had somehow forgotten that he'd already fed him earlier. "I'm not falling for that again, dog."

But then he tossed Ned a couple of his favorite treats. "Thanks for backing Moira up tonight. She might not appreciate our efforts, but I couldn't simply hang back and watch."

Because if Toby and that other guy hadn't come to their senses, she would have had her hands full on her own. He grabbed a couple of protein bars out of the pantry and a beer from the fridge, then headed for the sofa. Ned joined him, taking up far more room than one dog should. Titus turned on the news and settled back to unwind a little before heading to bed.

Stroking Ned's head helped with that. "I give it until tomorrow evening before Officer Fraser shows up to read me the riot act for getting involved. She has no idea how close I came to clocking Toby for shooting his mouth off about things getting rough for her."

He couldn't help but grin a little. "If that had happened, I have no doubt Jimmy wouldn't have been the only one sitting behind bars tonight. Think how much madder she'd be if she were to find out that Shay and I had planned ahead of time that he'd call me if he had to toss anyone out while Cade is gone."

Ned heaved a big sigh and rolled over. "Yeah, I know. It's not your problem."

When the phone rang, Titus considered ignoring it. Right now, he just wanted to kick back and relax for a while before turning in for the night. Sadly, he wouldn't be able to do that if he didn't check to see who was calling. Seeing Rita's name on the screen, he knew he had to answer. She wouldn't be calling for no reason, especially at this hour.

"Hey, Rita, what's up?"

A few seconds later, he had to ask her to back up and repeat about half of what she'd said. This time, she spoke at a more reasonable pace, but that didn't make the news any better. Realizing how stressed she sounded over having to abandon her post, he decided to lie. "No, I get it. Don't you worry about the café. I have names of a couple of people in town who said they might be willing to be on call in an emergency. Both of you go and help your sister. Once things settle, text me when you'll be heading back."

After asking her a few more questions, he said, "Let me know if it's a boy or a girl."

He should've foreseen the possibility of something like this happening when he hired the two sisters as his primary servers. The only person he knew in town who didn't have a regular job was Max Volkov. He had no idea if Max had ever worked in a restaurant, but Titus was willing to give him a crash course in the basics if he could come in for even a couple of hours until Titus could make other arrangements. Eyeing his companion, he asked, "Well, Ned, how do you feel about waiting tables?"

The dog opened his eyes briefly and then went right back to sleep.

"Yeah, that's what I thought."

CHAPTER FIVE

THE LAST THING Moira wanted to do first thing on her day off was to confront Titus Kondrat about the stunt he'd pulled the night before. No matter how good his intentions, she couldn't let something like that stand. She knew he was working, but what she wanted to tell him wouldn't take long, ten seconds tops. A simple "Don't ever do that again" would get the message across. Then maybe she could quit stewing about it and get on with her day.

When she reached the café, the line was out the door and halfway down the block. The place always did a brisk business during peak hours, but she couldn't remember seeing a backup like this. When she spotted a familiar face, she made her way through the crowd, promising those waiting that she wasn't cutting the line and would leave as soon as she asked someone a quick question. Mrs. Redd was actually her mother's friend, the one who sometimes stayed with Gram when both Moira and her mother had to be away from home.

When she tapped Mrs. Redd on the shoulder, the woman jumped. She'd been busy brushing something off her sleeve, frowning as she did so. "Moira, I didn't see you. I was just at a friend's house, and her cat shed all over me. I hope you're not hoping to cut in line. Well, unless you have to be on duty soon."

"No, I was just wondering why the line is so long this morning."

The older woman sighed. "Neither of the waitresses showed up for work today, so Mr. Kondrat is by himself. It's taken me thirty minutes to get this close to the door. To tell the truth, I'd go back home, but the special is his French toast. He makes it with challah bread, you know. It's delicious."

"I bet it is. Thanks for the information."

Moira retreated to a safer distance to consider what she could do to help the situation. It wasn't her problem, of course, but the café was the only place in town to get a meal. A fair number of the locals ate breakfast there before starting their workday. If they gave up and left, they'd either have to do without, go back home to eat, or else drive another twenty miles to the nearest diner.

Only one plan of action made sense. Titus might not like her poking her nose into his business any more than she'd appreciated his help last night, but too bad. She jogged down to the corner and headed for the back entrance of the café. One glance in the window only strengthened her resolve. It was total chaos.

When she let herself inside, the guy manning the grill didn't even glance in her direction. She approached him carefully, not wanting to startle him. "Gunner, where are the aprons?"

He pointed toward a drawer across the room. "You gonna work today?"

She nodded. "Yeah, I might be a bit rusty, but I'm pretty sure it will all come back to me. Does Titus use one of those fancy computer things to take orders or does he go old-school?"

Gunner laughed as he flipped fried eggs onto a plate. "Right now, the man wouldn't care if you carved the orders on stone tablets if it would get people served faster."

"Are the tables still numbered in the same order? One by the door and on around from there?"

"Yep."

First up, she made quick work of loading the dishwasher and setting it to run. That done, she picked up a pad of order slips, grabbed a couple of pens and then stuffed everything in her apron pocket. Spotting a rubber band, she slicked her hair back into a ponytail before washing her hands and heading out into the fray.

Before approaching any new customers, she decided delivering the backlog of orders sitting on the pass-through window should get priority. She loaded up a tray with the plates and added the packets of butter, bottles of syrup and other necessities.

"What do you think you're doing, Officer Fraser?"

"I'm helping out."

Titus nudged her aside with his hip to pick up the tray and grumbled, "Thanks, but I don't need any help."

So it was all right for him to poke his nose in her business last night, but not for her to offer to help him? "Yeah, you do, like it or not. And just so you know, I've put in way more hours working at this café than you have. I started busing tables here when I was fourteen and worked as a waitress during the summers all the way through high school and college."

She pointed toward the front window at the line of people still waiting to get in. "Those people need to get fed and soon."

With a look of pure frustration, he jerked his head in a nod. "Fine. Yell if you have questions."

As he stalked away, she set out another tray and repeated the same process. Titus came back for it within a couple of minutes. He didn't seem any happier about her being there, but he didn't say a word. When the backlog of orders was under control, she grabbed the cart that the servers used to clear tables after people had finished their meals. Despite the passage of years since she'd last worked at the café, evidently some skills didn't need to be relearned.

As she wiped down the last table, she noticed several people waiting near the door. On her way toward them, she gathered up several stacks of menus that were scattered around the room and returned them to the bin where they belonged.

Pasting on a smile, she asked the people at the front of the line, "How many?"

"Four, Moira."

"This way."

Titus glared at her from across the room, but she ignored him and returned for the next group. Once she had all the tables filled again, she started a fresh pot of coffee before taking the previous one with her as she circled the room topping off drinks for customers between taking orders from those who were waiting.

"Officer Fraser, a moment of your time, please."

Moira came to an abrupt stop next to where Otto Klaus was sitting. "Mr. Mayor, what can I do for you?"

"You're supposed to be in charge of the police department. Shouldn't you be doing that job instead of busing tables? That's not what we're paying you for."

She forced a smile. "Actually, it's my day off, although I still check in on a regular basis. The other officers know to call if they need backup. When I saw the line outside, I figured Mr. Kondrat might need a little help."

Otto didn't look any happier. "I hope Titus is grateful. I hear tell Rita Leoni and her sister Beth left to help their older sister. Seems she went into labor early."

So that's what had happened.

"Is there anything else I can get you? More coffee?"

Otto waved her off. "I'd like my check."

"I'll let Titus know."

She caught up with the man in question a second later. "The mayor would like his bill."

He studied her for a second. "Did he say something to upset you?"

"Seems he thought I was blowing off my real job to work here." Seeing the flare of anger in his expression, she stepped in front of him. "It's not your problem, and I already set him straight."

When his expression relaxed, she asked, "So should I take orders, bus tables or wash dishes?"

He glanced around the room. "If you'll take orders, I'll deliver the food and run the register."

"Sounds good."

Before she could walk away, he grabbed her arm just long enough to stop her. "Thanks for doing this, Moira."

She pointed a finger at him. "I'm still mad about last night, but you're welcome."

His mouth quirked up in a small smile. "Fair enough."

IT WASN'T UNTIL ten thirty that Titus finally had a chance to catch his breath. to make sure Moira and Gunner also got a break, he locked the front door and posted a handwritten note that the café would reopen sometime between eleven and eleven thirty. He'd barely sat down at his usual table in the back corner when Moira walked out of the kitchen and headed in his direction.

She plunked down two plates containing sandwiches and cups of soup and then walked away. A few seconds later, she was back with glasses of water and two slices of pie. Without asking permission, she sat down across from him. When Titus didn't dive right in, she pushed the plate closer to him. "Eat while you can. Things will pick up speed again all too soon."

A wise man knew when to argue and when to accept his marching orders. "Yes, ma'am."

Apparently satisfied that he was taken care of, Moira picked up her own sandwich and took a big bite. It was hard not to stare as she took pleasure in the simple act of eating. The truth was there was so much he admired about Moira even if the mad rush they'd dealt with had left its mark. Her ponytail was a bit bedraggled. There was also a grease stain on her apron and a smudge of what was probably flour on her cheek. She'd never looked more beautiful to him, not that he was about to tell her that.

The woman was already mad at him. No use in making matters worse.

They ate in companionable silence. She wasn't wrong. He needed to refuel before people started arriving for lunch. The breakfast rush lasted way longer than normal because he hadn't been able to find anyone to fill in for Rita and her sister. If Moira hadn't shown up out of the blue, it would have been a total disaster.

Never in his wildest dreams would he have ever expected Moira to be the one who would ride to the rescue. He owed her big-time, which reminded him… "I'll need you to fill out some paperwork."

She frowned at him. "What kind of paperwork?"

"So I can pay you for today."

"Nope, no paperwork. For one thing, you haven't even asked if I have an up-to-date food handler's card."

The thought hadn't even occurred to him. That could be problematic if the health inspector found out. "I don't suppose you do."

Feeling a bit smug, she pulled out her wallet. "And you would be wrong. I used to volunteer at a local soup kitchen in Seattle, so my card is current."

That simplified things, although he wasn't above bending a few rules if it meant his customers got fed. Meanwhile, she pointed at him with her fork. "Besides, as the mayor so graciously pointed out, I already have a job. I was just helping out my friends and neighbors."

Now, that was an interesting thought. "So now we're friends?"

It was hard not to laugh at the shocked expression on Moira's face. Before she could sputter out an answer, he stopped her. "Never mind. I know you didn't do it for me. You took an oath to serve and protect. I just didn't realize the *serve* part referred to French toast and coffee."

"Not funny, Titus."

For some reason, sparring with her gave him a new boost of energy. He might just make it through the day after all. "Yeah, it is, but I'm still grateful. If you won't let me pay you for your time, at least let me reward your efforts with the pie of your choice. I won't have time to bake it today, but I promise I'm good for it."

She was already shaking her head. "You've already fed me lunch. That's enough."

"Okay, chocolate-cream it is. I'll even throw in a couple of those cherry mini pies for your mom and grandmother so you don't have to share."

It was fun watching the by-the-book cop warring with temptation. "Fine. I'll take a pie and the mini ones for Gram and my mom."

With that settled, he finished off his meal, taking his time because he knew the second they finished eating she would rip into him about last night. As it turned out, he was wrong about that. She didn't wait that long.

"Titus, last night cannot happen again. Civilians getting involved in police business, no matter how well intentioned, is a recipe for trouble. If you had gone vigilante on those guys, the repercussions would have been serious for both of us. And what if Ned bit one of them? You could have ended up being ordered to have him put down for being a vicious animal."

He swallowed hard at the thought of that prospect. She was right. That didn't bear thinking about. He'd jeopardized Ned without meaning to.

Meanwhile, Moira met his gaze head-on, something few people were comfortable doing. "If you doubt my abilities as a cop, especially in public, other people will as well. Cade trusted me to do the job. Take your lead from him."

He leaned back in his chair, feeling pretty darn defensive by that point. "I never once said you couldn't handle your job."

Moira's pretty face was now set in hard lines. "Then why were you there last night?"

"I was out walking Ned."

She snorted, giving his weak excuse all the respect it deserved. "Fine, you were walking your dog and just happened to end up in a stare-down contest with those three drunken truckers. Regardless, no more, Mr. Kondrat. Do you understand?"

Rather than answer her question, he asked one of his own. "Any reason you've reverted to calling me by my last name? I'd think after everything we've been through in the past few days, we'd be on a first-name basis."

Moira was getting more exasperated with him by the second. She shoved her empty plate to the side and leaned forward, forearms on the table. "Fine. Titus, don't follow me around when I'm on duty. I'd hate to have to toss you in a cell for interfering in police business, but don't think I won't."

He mirrored her position, narrowing the distance between them. "Does that mean it's okay if I follow you around when you aren't on duty?"

Her eyes flared wide and then narrowed. "Are you making fun of me?"

It was hard not to laugh at her outrage. "Absolutely not. Just asking for clarification."

"Let's keep it simple. Don't follow me around—period."

Then she stood and gathered up their dirty dishes. Jerking her head in the direction of the door, she said, "Looks like people heard about the backup this morning and decided to get in line early. Do you want me to start seating people and get their drinks while you take orders?"

"Sounds like a plan, but are you sure you want to spend your whole day here with me?"

After setting their dishes on the cart, she gathered up a stack of menus and headed for the door. "You'd be surprised what I'd be willing to do to get my very own chocolate-cream pie."

Okay, that put a whole lot of thoughts in Titus's head that he had no business thinking about her. Definitely time to change the subject. "Just so you know, Max Volkov should be here any minute now. He said he could bus tables and wash dishes."

"That's nice of him."

Titus wasn't so sure. "That depends on how many dishes he breaks. Seems that's why he got fired after only a week at his last restaurant job."

He started to walk away but then turned

back. "By the way, don't mention the pie to him. I'm guessing you remember when Max first showed up in Dunbar and claimed the Trillium Nugget belonged to his family instead of the historical museum down the street. The whole town was up in arms over his attempt to make off with that big chunk of gold, Dunbar's most prized possession."

She looked a bit puzzled about where he was headed with this. "Yeah, it was quite the deal."

Titus grinned at her. "Well, I told Max he owed me free labor for letting him hang out here at the café back when everyone else in town hated him."

She was still laughing as she opened the door and let the waiting horde rush in.

THE REST OF the day passed in a blur. Moira had forgotten how exhausting standing on her feet all day could be. At least she'd had on her running shoes when she'd thrown herself into the fray to help feed what felt like the entire population of Dunbar. When Titus finally locked the front door and turned off the lights in the dining room, her poor feet were screaming in protest.

Max was still finishing up the last of the dishes when she took a seat at the same table where she and her grandmother had enjoyed their pie the other night. There wasn't anything left for her to do around the café, but she didn't have the energy to walk back home. She'd asked Max for a lift, but he'd walked to the café, too. Upon hearing that, Titus had offered to drive her home once he took care of a few more things. She didn't want to ask her mother to come get her since that would mean leaving Gram on her own. Neither of them liked to do that even for a short time. Since Carli was working tonight, that wasn't an option, either.

In the end, she'd reluctantly accepted Titus's offer. She sipped a cup of tea while the man started prepping things for the next day. At least he'd managed to hire some temporary help to cover until Rita and her sister returned. Max put up the last of the clean dishes and then took a seat across from Moira.

"Whew, I don't know if I could ever get used to working at this pace full-time."

She smiled at him. "You get used to it after a while, but it's why I always leave a big tip when I eat out."

He looked around. "With my new appreciation for how hard everyone works here, I'm going to up the ante when I tip from now on."

"My staff will appreciate it." Titus picked up two plates and headed their way. "I figured both of you could use a little something to eat about now."

After setting down the plates, he immediately snatched them back up and switched them around. "Sorry about that. The salad without the nuts is Moira's. She's allergic to them. The last thing she needs is another trip to the emergency room for a shot to counter the effects."

Max picked up his fork and dug right in. "Good catch."

Moira started to do the same, but then it hit her that she'd never ordered anything that had contained nuts here at the café, or even mentioned her allergies to the staff. The problem wasn't particularly life-threatening, but she preferred not to take any chances. The real question was how Titus knew that she needed to avoid nuts, much less that she'd ended up in the emergency room not long after she became a police officer.

Rather than ask questions in front of Max,

she ate her salad and quietly watched Titus as he went back to chopping veggies. A few more pieces of the puzzle he represented started falling into place even if others didn't seem to fit at all. Once they were alone, though, she would demand some answers.

At that moment, he glanced back over his shoulder and winced before quickly turning away when he saw her watching him. Oh, yeah, that man was hiding something, and she had just realized what it was.

The night she'd gone to the ER, she hadn't driven herself there. No, someone else had rushed her to a nearby hospital—Ryan Donovan, her erstwhile boyfriend at the time. Not even her mother knew about that evening because she worried enough about Moira being on her own in the big city. Instead, Moira had told her mother a different part of the truth— that her doctor had recommended that she get some allergy testing done and discovered that she had a mild problem with nuts.

Max finished off his salad and put his plate and silverware in the dishwasher. "I'm heading out, Titus, but let me know if you need me again."

Turning back to Moira, he smiled at her.

"When I called my wife to tell her that I'd be later than expected, she said to remind you that the book club will be meeting at our house the week after Shelby and Cade get back."

"Tell Rikki I'll be there unless I have to work."

"I will. 'Night, you two."

Moira waited until Max was gone before getting up to lock the door. This next conversation needed to be private. When she turned back around, Titus was once again leaning against the counter with his arms crossed over his chest, doing his best to look relaxed. However, she'd learned a lot about reading body language over the course of her career. To a casual observer, Titus might look cool, calm and collected, but there was a lot of tension in his shoulders and panic in the depths of those deep brown eyes.

Positioning herself a few feet in front of him, she met his gaze head-on. "Ordinarily I would now ask how you happen to know about my allergies. But all things considered, I don't have to, seeing as you're not Titus Kondrat at all."

She prowled a few steps closer, a mix of

anger and betrayal feeding her fury. "So tell me, Ryan Donovan, how long have you been out of prison?"

CHAPTER SIX

TITUS KNEW MOIRA had finally connected all the dots, but having that name flung in his face still came as a shock. It sure had taken her long enough to see through the surface changes in his appearance to recognize the man she used to know, maybe even loved. Heaven knew he'd been dreading this moment, but somehow it also came with a huge dose of relief. He doubted she felt the same.

"So, Moira, it's been a while. I guess I owe you an apology. I never meant—"

The sudden chill in the room had nothing to do with the setting on the thermostat and everything to do with the hard-eyed, furious woman glaring at him. She cut him off with a slash of her hand. "Don't play nice now. I bet you've been having a big laugh behind my back, so I don't want an apology. Not from you, especially not now. An explanation might be nice, though."

Her face was flushed, but he didn't know if it was temper or embarrassment that accounted for those rosy cheeks. He'd never meant to hurt her, and the last thing he'd ever do was laugh at her. Ned had been dozing in his bed, but now he was up and moving. The dog positioned himself between Moira and Titus, as if unsure which one of them needed his protection right now.

Titus stroked the dog's head, desperately needing that small connection to help keep himself grounded in the moment. "I've never laughed at you, Moira. And if I could have told you the truth back then, I would have."

"What? They don't let prisoners write letters these days? Or make phone calls or send emails?"

Stubborn woman. "I couldn't contact you at the time without putting people at risk, myself included."

She stared at him for the longest time. "Why? Did you rat out your low-life associates?"

"In a manner of speaking."

"Don't play word games with me. Not now."

"You're right." Knowing this moment had been bound to come sooner or later, he'd prepared for it. "Give me a minute. I'll be right back."

Without waiting for her response, Titus headed for the staircase that led up to his office on the second floor. He should have known she wouldn't do as he said. She walked into the room before he'd even had time to unlock the file cabinet. He pulled out the manila envelope he kept tucked all the way in the back.

Turning to face her, he reluctantly held it out to her. "Your answer is in there."

She dumped the contents out of the envelope onto his desk. After staring at the worn leather wallet for a second or two, she slowly picked it up and then looked at the badge and picture inside. She held it up to the light to study the ID photo and then ran her finger over the badge as if to verify it wasn't plastic. Such a distrustful woman, but then she had good reason to be.

Her expression was incredulous when she finally asked, "You're DEA?"

"Make that past tense. I haven't been for a long while now, especially since my cover was blown."

She abruptly shoved the contents back into

the envelope, then tossed it on his desk. "Is that why you look so different?"

Moira waved her hand toward his head and down to his feet. "Your hair is dark, not almost blond, and your blue eyes have magically turned brown. You're a lot more muscular, and you've picked up all those tats along the way. You don't even sound the same."

She didn't know the half of it. "When you saw me get taken away in cuffs, the goal was to preserve my cover as Ryan Donovan. It didn't work, however. Although the task force rounded up most members of the drug ring that night, a few had slipped through the cracks. They caught up with me a short time later and expressed their displeasure."

Her face turned pale. "How badly were you hurt?"

"Collapsed lung, shattered kneecap, broken ribs, internal bleeding." He rubbed his hand over his nose and cheeks. "Multiple facial fractures. The doctors worked from pictures to piece everything back together. They came pretty close to getting it right."

He tried not to think about that period of his life much. It had taken time, but his injuries had eventually healed. Mostly, anyway. When she didn't immediately speak, he filled the silence himself. "I walked away from the DEA and went to culinary school. The rest is history."

She flinched, as if his words had cut her to the quick. "Like me?"

He sighed. "No, never you, Moira. Like I already said, I would've clued you in back then if it wouldn't have put you and others in danger."

"And in the ten years since?"

"All things considered, I thought it best to let you get on with your life."

Her temper flashed hot. "It wasn't solely your decision to make. I should've had a say. Maybe not when the drug bust went down. I get that, but what about later, once the dust settled? Well, unless everything you claimed to feel about me, about us…was a lie."

She clenched her hands into white-knuckled fists. "Tell me, Agent Kondrat, was I only another piece of your cover story?"

Now he was getting angry. She hadn't been the only one left hurting ten years ago. Walking away from her had cost both of them a lot of pain. "I never lied to you, not about anything that mattered."

Her answering snort said it all. "Do you expect me to believe that when you lied about virtually everything I knew about you? Heck, I don't even know your real name."

She drew a ragged breath, still fighting for control. "I thought it was bad enough dealing with the knowledge that I was a cop who fell hard for a charming criminal. It's so much worse finding out that the man I cared about wasn't even real."

By that point, her blue eyes were bright with tears. Knowing he'd made this strong woman cry was a real gut punch. "I use my real name these days. Ryan Donovan was a persona the DEA created for me to use when we were working to bring down that drug ring. When you and I met, I'd already been undercover for more than a year working my way up the food chain."

She poked an accusing finger into his chest. "I told you I was a cop that night at that dance club. You had to know that would complicate things for both of us. Why didn't you walk away then?"

Titus caught her hand before she could

poke him a second time. "Honestly, if I'd had a lick of sense, I would have."

He wanted to brush away the tears trickling down her cheeks, but dropped his hand down when she jerked back out of his reach. "Trouble was, I didn't want to."

She wasn't buying it, but it was nothing less than the truth. Back then, there was something about her that had drawn him like no other woman had ever been able to do. He'd been foolish enough to think they could share a few laughs and then he would walk away, no harm, no foul. Instead, he'd hurt the only woman who'd ever mattered to him and all but destroyed himself in the process.

"How did you end up in Dunbar, of all places?"

Okay, that one was tricky. She was already mad at him. He'd thrown the dice and bet everything on rebuilding his life in her hometown just so he might someday have this very conversation with her. Clearly, telling her that wasn't going to go over well at all. It was proof positive he wasn't firing on all cylinders when it came to anything to do with Moira.

"After I left the DEA, I went to culinary school. After gaining some experience, I wanted to buy a café. This one was on the market and fit my requirements."

That earned him a huge eye roll. "Which were?"

He ticked the reasons off on his fingers— at least those he could safely share. "Small town, updated kitchen, steady clientele and close to Seattle."

"And you're asking me to believe the fact that it was my hometown didn't enter into your decision."

Okay, that wasn't something he particularly wanted to admit to, but leave it to Moira to jump to the right conclusion. "Yes, Moira, I picked Dunbar because it was your hometown. I figured we'd run into each other eventually."

"Well, now we have. I hope you're happy. I'm not."

After one more glare hot enough to melt the polar ice caps, she did an abrupt about-face, then marched back downstairs and out the door, slamming it hard enough to rattle the windows. He shoved the envelope back in the file cabinet and locked it. Ned was waiting for him at the bottom of the steps, his head cocked to the side as if asking what Titus had done to upset his new friend.

Now wasn't the time for long explanations. "Come on, dog. We need to make sure she gets home in one piece."

As soon as they were out the door, they took off at a dead run. It might have been faster to drive, but he doubted she'd get in the truck with him. Instead, he and Ned kept a fast pace, heading in the general direction of her mother's house. He finally stopped when he realized Moira was nowhere in sight. There were several routes she could've taken, and the woman could really move when she wanted to. Luckily, he had Ned as his secret weapon. "Find her for me, boy."

The dog immediately put his nose to the ground and ranged back and forth until he finally caught her scent. He woofed softly and turned off the main road onto a side street. Sure enough, Titus spotted her two blocks ahead. He kicked it into high gear, determined to reach her before she could take shelter inside her house.

They needed to talk, and neither of them needed an audience.

Moira glanced back in their direction and

then picked up the pace as well. That didn't keep him from gaining on her. She was a fast runner, but his longer legs trumped her speed. When he caught up with her, he blocked her way. She tried to step around him, but he wasn't ready to give up.

"You have to be tired, Moira. At least let me walk you home."

"I'm perfectly capable of getting there on my own."

"Never said you couldn't."

Under normal circumstances, the woman was more than capable of taking care of herself. But right now, thanks to him, she was both tired and upset. He doubted she was more than marginally aware of their surroundings. Shortening his stride to match hers, he stepped aside and let Moira set the pace for now.

A few steps later, without so much as glancing at him, she asked, "Does Cade know about your past? About us?"

"Absolutely not. What happened between you and me is nobody's business but ours. As to the rest, Cade probably has his suspicions about my former employment, and I've been thinking about telling him the truth. The man knows how to keep a secret, and I don't want my past becoming public knowledge."

She shot him a quick look. "Why?"

"Because there are still a few people out there who have long memories and a taste for revenge."

Before he could stop himself, he rubbed his throat. As soon as he realized what he was doing, he dropped his hand back down to his side, but not before she noticed. "The same ones who are responsible for why your voice sounds so rough these days?"

"Yeah."

Not that he wanted to talk about it. During the fight, his voice box had been permanently damaged. The doctors hadn't been sure if that last part was from actual physical trauma or from him screaming so much. It was just another in a long list of bad experiences he'd just as soon forget about. To his surprise, Moira reached out to squeeze his hand. "I'm sorry."

"Not your fault. I got careless."

They were now in sight of her family home. He slowed down, pretty sure she wouldn't want her mother or neighbors seeing him escorting her to the front door. "Thank you again for helping out today."

"I didn't do it for you."

No, she'd done it for her friends and neighbors. The woman had a generous heart.

Unfortunately, he seriously doubted that generosity would be extended to him in the near future, if ever. That was probably for the best. It would make it easier for him to maintain some distance from her. When he'd moved to Dunbar, he'd hoped they could eventually be friends, but now he wasn't sure that mere friendship would ever be enough. "I'll let you know when I have your pies ready."

Moira shook her head. "Forget it. I don't want them."

She wasn't the only one with a stubborn streak. "You'll get them, anyway. I bet your mom won't turn them down. She'd probably think that would be rude. Your grandmother wouldn't for sure. She likes my pies."

He risked a small grin. "In fact, I think she likes me, period. She's also quite fond of Ned."

Apparently, Moira didn't find his assessment of his standing with her family amusing. "That's because they don't know the truth about you. Mom might not know all of the details, but she does know that I went through a bad breakup back in the day. If she found out that it was you, she'd come after you with her rolling pin."

"So that's where you get your fire." He fought the urge to brush back a lock of hair that had escaped her ponytail. "All things considered, I'd probably let her give it her best shot."

Moira didn't respond, but she patted Ned on the head, giving him a quick scratch. "Thanks for seeing me home, Ned. You might have questionable taste in owners, but you're a good dog."

Turning her attention back to him, she said, "As for you, keep your distance. Not just now, but for the foreseeable future. Whatever we once shared wasn't real, because the man I thought you were never existed. I was in love with a ghost."

Okay, enough was enough. He might have had secrets that he couldn't share at the time, but how he'd felt about her hadn't been a lie. If their relationship, however fleeting, hadn't been so incredibly special, they wouldn't both be hurting so much right now. Maybe it was time to remind them both of that fact. Moving in too quickly for Moira to escape, he caught her in his arms and pulled her in close to his chest. He was several inches over six feet, while she was about five-ten. That made her short enough to tuck under his chin when they slow-danced, but tall enough to kiss without having to bend down too far. He'd always loved how well they fit together. "What we shared was real all right, Moira. Otherwise, losing it wouldn't have hurt so much."

Defiant to the end, she met his gaze without flinching. "You were pretending to be a man you weren't, so you were only playing a part in a play. Nothing was real."

"Yeah, it was. So is this."

Keeping his hold on her gentle, he moved slowly. If she'd wanted to break free, she could have. Instead, she watched him as he closed the last bit of distance between them. When he kissed her, it was as if the past ten years had never happened. At first, she didn't give in to the moment, but gradually Moira softened in his arms as he gently coaxed rather than demanded her cooperation. He'd always wondered if he'd only imagined the way she could bring him to his knees with a simple kiss. Now he knew the truth. This woman had laid claim to his heart and never given it back.

Not that there was anything simple about this kiss, which tasted of lost love and so many regrets.

Then without warning, she jerked free of his embrace and immediately wiped the back of her hand across her mouth. Did she actually think that would erase the reality of what had just happened? The defiant gesture would have infuriated him if he hadn't seen the slight tremor in her hand before she could hide it.

"Like I said, Kondrat, stay away from me. I have enough on my plate right now without you playing mind games with me."

Then she walked away, her head held high, and never once looked back in his direction. He waited until she let herself into the house before heading back toward the café. He was bone-tired and ached from head to toe after the emotional wringer he'd just been through. Regardless, right now sleep would be beyond him. Too many memories and too many regrets running rampant in his head. Better to take out his frustration on innocent vegetables rather than lie in bed, staring up at the ceiling.

When Ned tried to turn toward home, Titus didn't stop him. "Go ahead, boy. I'll be along eventually."

Then he walked off alone, as usual.

CHAPTER SEVEN

MOIRA CHECKED HER appearance in the mirror over her dresser. Her hair was swept up in a high ponytail, her makeup mostly hid the dark circles under her eyes and her uniform was neat and tidy. Although she couldn't quite put a finger on the reason why, she still felt as if she was a cartoon cop made from pieces of construction paper pasted together by a small child with a whimsical sense of humor.

Last evening, she'd burned through what little energy she'd had left trying to maintain some semblance of normalcy in front of her family. Even though she'd done her best to pretend that everything was fine, her all-too-perceptive mom had realized that something was wrong. Moira had waved off her concern, claiming that she was simply tired after being on her feet all day. After all, it had been years since she'd put in a full day working in the café. At least the news that Titus intended to pay her with pie had proved to be enough of a distraction to avoid any more unwanted questions.

Even going to bed early hadn't done much to replenish her depleted energy level. That probably had more to do with the emotional toll of learning the truth about what had happened to Ryan...or Titus—whoever he was. How could she have so totally misread the situation? Granted, she'd barely been out of the police academy at the time, but there had to have been some clues that she'd missed that all wasn't as it had seemed.

For one thing, she hadn't heard anything about him standing trial, not that she'd expected to have to testify. After all, she and her fellow officers had been at the big drug bust solely to do traffic control. It had only been by happenstance that she'd been in the perfect position to watch Ryan being dragged out in cuffs along with his low-life buddies. Even now, so many years later, she could remember the bitter heartbreak and disgust she'd felt as it all played out like a bad movie.

As the man she loved had passed right by her, he kept his eyes pinned firmly on the ground, never once glancing in her direction.

At least he'd given her that much. None of her coworkers knew anything about the man she'd been dating, only that he'd left town suddenly with no explanation. Carli was the only one who knew the truth. Well, most of it, anyway. Moira only had vague memories of the night she'd poured out her troubles to her friend as she and Carli overindulged in pizza, washed down with copious amounts of wine. Her hangover the next day had been one for the record books.

As tempting as it was to see if her friend was available for another girls' night of whining and wine, Moira couldn't risk it right now. Her emotions were too raw, and Carli already suspected there was something simmering between Moira and Titus. She'd be sure to read far too much into the fact that Moira had let him kiss her brains out last night. Besides, one drink too many would increase the chances of the truth of Titus's past slipping out. She might be furious with him and all the deception, but she was a cop to the core. There was no way she would put a former officer's life at risk because of hurt feelings.

She picked up her service belt and strapped it on before retrieving her weapon from the small gun safe in her bedside table. As ready as she'd ever be, she headed into the kitchen to grab a couple of protein bars to eat on the way to the office. It wouldn't be much of a breakfast, but the last thing she wanted this morning was to sit down at the table with her mother. The woman had an uncanny knack for accurately reading Moira's mood. If she thought someone had upset her daughter, the woman was likely to go on the warpath.

She'd almost made it to the door when her grandmother walked into the kitchen. "Morning, Moira. Off to work already?"

"Yes, I have some paperwork to take care of before I go out on patrol." She noticed Gram looked more like her old self. She'd taken the time to neatly style her hair and even put on a little makeup. "How are you feeling this morning?"

Her grandmother rolled her eyes. "More clearheaded than usual if that's what you're asking."

She stopped talking, then poured herself a cup of coffee and continued, "Clearheaded enough that I could tell you were pretty upset when you got home last night, even though you tried hard to hide it from your mom."

Pointing out the window, she changed subjects without waiting to see if Moira would offer up an explanation. "By the way, I happened to be looking outside when you walked up to the house. It was hard not to notice that you had an escort out there waiting and watching to make sure you made it inside without a problem."

It was surprising Gram hadn't mentioned that last night. Regardless, Moira didn't want to have this conversation. It was a huge relief when her grandmother finally looked in her direction. "I'm pretty sure that was Ned out there standing guard. Does his owner know you borrowed his dog?"

At least Gram hadn't seen Titus, which was a huge relief. "I didn't ask him to follow me home from the café. He decided to do that all on his own. Besides, I'm not sure that dog thinks he's actually owned by anyone."

Her grandmother huffed a small laugh. "You're probably right about that. Did I hear you tell your mother that Titus is paying you with pies for helping him out at the café yesterday?"

"Yeah, he insisted he owed me something

when I refused to let him offer me any money. I didn't do it to earn extra cash."

Gram moved on to making herself some toast. "A man like him has a sense of pride. He probably doesn't want to be beholden to anyone."

That was very likely true.

She kissed her grandmother on the cheek. "Have a good day, Gram. I've got to hit the road."

Gram set her cup on the table and followed Moira to the door, grabbing her hand to keep her from leaving just yet. "I know you love your job, honey, but you need more in your life than being a cop. I've always suspected something happened back when you first joined the force that left you a little gun-shy in the romance department. Since you stayed in law enforcement, I have to think that it didn't happen on the job. But whatever it was, it changed you."

She gave Moira's hand a quick squeeze before releasing it. "Life can get pretty lonely when you don't have someone special waiting for you at the end of the day. I miss your grandpa every day, and your mother feels the same about your dad. Just ask her."

Her smile turned a little wicked and her faded blue eyes sparked with mischief. "You could do a lot worse than a man who knows how to cook and loves his dog. I shouldn't have to point out that Mr. Kondrat isn't hard on the eyes, either. There's something about those broad shoulders and tattoos."

Then she giggled like a schoolgirl. "I'm just saying."

Before Moira could do much more than sputter at her outrageous behavior, Gram walked out of the room. Sadly, she sincerely wished she could say her grandmother was wrong, but it never paid to lie to herself. The Ryan Donovan iteration of the man she'd known ten years ago had been sophisticated and handsome enough to grace the cover of any fashion magazine. Whenever the two of them had gone out, he'd drawn the attention of women as they passed by.

The Titus Kondrat version, though, was far rougher around the edges. It was more than the gravel in his voice or the tattoos, although they were part of it. Life had left its mark on him in other ways. There was an edginess to him that ran bone-deep, especially when he tore through town on that big Harley he liked to ride. At the same time, the man could be surprisingly gentle when the occasion called for it, just like when he'd gallantly escorted her grandmother from the café and helped her into Moira's vehicle.

That stood out in stark contrast to the night outside the bar when Titus took exception to the three truckers threatening Moira. On that occasion, he'd worn a veneer of barely leashed violence like a second skin. She might not have appreciated him interfering in police business, but she couldn't deny that she was drawn to his alpha-male nature on some level.

Not that she'd ever admit that to anyone, especially the man himself. The situation was too complicated—he was too complicated. His ability to switch personas was a good reminder that he wasn't to be trusted. There was no way to know what was real and what wasn't. She couldn't bet her heart on a man she couldn't trust.

After glancing at the time on the kitchen clock, she hustled out the door. While she wasn't going to be late for her shift, she wanted to get there early enough to clear out some paperwork before she was due on patrol again.

When Moira walked into the office, Oscar was working at the front desk. He smiled and pointed to a paper bag sitting on the counter. Her name had been scribbled across the front in felt-tip pen. There was a matching one sitting next to it with Oscar's name on it.

"That Kondrat fella dropped those by a little while ago. Since we're all putting in extra hours with Cade gone, he thought we might appreciate a treat. I put the others in the fridge, but I knew you were on your way in."

If the gift had come from anyone else, she would've been pleased by the gesture. But she was pretty sure this wasn't Titus being thoughtful. No, this was him messing with her. It was tempting to toss the bag in the trash, but that would only have Oscar asking questions she didn't want to answer, especially because the older officer was known to share juicy tidbits of gossip with Bea at the bakeshop down the street. From there, the information would make the rounds from one end of town to the other with lightning speed. After that, the phone calls would start, and no one needed that kind of grief.

It was time to get down to business. "Anything I need to know about?"

"Nothing much going on other than the usual speeding tickets and such." Then Oscar frowned. "We have gotten a couple more reports involving missing pets. No evidence of foul play, so they could have wandered off. Maybe coyotes got them. That happens once in a while. I told the people to reach out to local shelters and to post flyers around town."

"That's pretty much all anyone can do." She finally picked up the paper bag. "I'll be in Cade's office if you need me. Then I'll be heading out on patrol in an hour."

"I made a pot of fresh coffee if you want some."

Moira grimaced as she walked away. She could use some caffeine about now, but the truth was that Oscar's coffee was a little too high-octane for her taste. Still, it was better than nothing. She stopped in the break room to pour herself a cup, adding extra sugar and cream to mellow out the acid brew.

When she was safely ensconced in Cade's office with the door closed, she finally opened the bag Titus had dropped off. When she saw that it was a sandwich, a bag of chips and a couple of sugar cookies, she breathed a sigh of relief. So maybe she'd been wrong about him messing with her. Regardless of his intent, she knew the food in the bag would be one heck of a lot better than the protein bars she still hadn't eaten.

Rather than save the meal for later, she decided to dive right in. After setting aside the cookies to snack on while on patrol, she opened the bag of salt-and-vinegar potato chips. It was most irritating that Titus had remembered that was her favorite flavor, just like he still knew how she liked her tea. That didn't mean she wasn't going to eat them; it would be a shame to let them go to waste. She munched on the chips between returning a few phone calls.

Once she caught up on those, she unwrapped the paper on the sandwich far enough to see what kind it was. It turned out to be turkey and Swiss cheese on a brioche bun, no tomato, no onion and light on the mayo. Now the jerk was just showing off, not that it would stop her from eating every bite. It wasn't until she finished removing the wrapper completely that she realized Titus had written her a note on the inside of it.

Rather than read it immediately, she folded the paper back up and stuck it in her pocket to deal with later. It wasn't as if she even cared what the man had to say. She had no intention of getting involved with Titus again and had made that very clear to him last night. She'd even almost convinced herself that it was the wisest course of action. Her time would be far better spent concentrating on her job. With that in mind, she made quick work of the sandwich because she had files to update, people to serve, a job to do.

About halfway through the first file she tried to read, she gave up and set it aside. There was no way she could focus on the work at hand with that stupid wrapper burning a hole in her pocket. Grumbling under her breath, she pulled the note back out and gingerly unfolded it on top of the desk.

After skimming over it, she growled under her breath as she started over at the top and read it more slowly. Her emotions bounced all over the place, running both hot and cold, as she absorbed the brief message.

I know you don't want to hear it and maybe don't believe it, but I am sorry about what happened between us. Who knows, maybe someday you might even forgive me. For now, enjoy your meal. If you're reading this, at least you didn't throw it away. I figured that was a distinct possibility, but you always were a sucker for salt-and-vinegar chips. Be safe.

Titus

Sorry now that she'd given her curiosity free rein, she wadded up the wrapper and tossed it in the trash. An hour later, she finished the last report and logged off the computer. It was time to start her patrol. Before heading out to the parking lot, she filled her thermos with coffee and tucked the cookies she'd saved from earlier into her pocket to eat later.

She made it halfway to the parking lot before doing an abrupt about-face and marching back into Cade's office to retrieve the note from the trash. Despite her best efforts, she couldn't convince herself that she only did so to prevent anyone else from finding it. If that was true, she could've simply shredded the darn thing. Instead, she read it over one last time before folding it neatly and stashing it in her jacket pocket.

Maybe Titus was truly sorry for hurting her; it wasn't as if she knew what went on in that man's head these days. Regardless, it didn't change anything. Not really. They'd both moved on, started new jobs, built new lives. All that was left of their shared past was a mix of memories, both good and bad. Nothing that was worth losing sleep over. Eventually they'd figure out how to live life in a small town without getting in each other's way. It shouldn't be that hard. All it would take was a little effort on both their parts. Easy-peasy, no sweat.

And maybe if she kept repeating that, she might eventually believe it. On that happy note, she headed out to stand guard over the citizens of Dunbar.

TWO NIGHTS LATER, she was back out on the road and bored out of her mind. Mostly, she was happy to have an uneventful shift. Other times, though, it felt as if she was driving in circles and accomplishing nothing. For one thing, it was hard to vary her route very much in a town with only six hundred people. There were also a few places that she made a point of checking on more frequently than others. Shay Barnaby's bar was definitely at the top of that list, but there hadn't been any notable trouble there since the night Shay had given Jimmy and his buddies the boot.

Maybe it was because Jimmy's antics had ended with him spending a few nights behind bars. Somehow, Moira thought it was more likely because he and his two drunken companions had also been banned from both the bar and Titus's café for the foreseeable future. Nobody wanted to have their name on that list.

As she did a quick turn through the neighborhood where her family lived, Moira spotted her mother's friend walking along the sidewalk. It seemed odd for Mrs. Redd to be walking that late at night, so Moira slowed to a stop and rolled down the passenger-side window.

"Hey, Mrs. Redd, is everything okay? Do you need a lift home?"

The older woman had been facing away from Moira. When she turned around, she was holding a cat. "Oh, hi, Moira. Everything is fine. I was too restless to sleep and thought a little fresh air would help."

Moira pointed toward the calico kitty. "Who's your friend?"

Mrs. Redd stroked the cat's head several times before setting it back down on the ground. The animal took off like a shot, disappearing into the bushes next to the closest house. "I don't know her name, but she must live close by. I see her fairly often when I walk by here."

She smiled at Moira. "I guess I should head home myself."

"The offer of a ride is still open."

Mrs. Redd shook her head and started walking. "It's not far and the exercise will do me good. Tell your mother and grandmother I said hi."

"Will do."

Moira slowly pulled away, still keeping an eye on Mrs. Redd in the rearview mirror. She lived on the next street and should be all right for that short distance. Regardless, Moira decided she'd circle the block to make sure Mrs. Redd arrived home safely.

Ten minutes later, Moira headed for the two-lane highway that led into town to watch for late-evening speeders. When she reached the spot where she liked to set up shop, she backed into position. She'd barely gotten situated when a huge pickup truck went roaring past. She clocked the nitwit at thirty over the limit. Flipping on her lights and siren, she hit the gas to pull back out onto the highway.

That's when things went horribly wrong.

Her left front tire hit a deep pothole she missed seeing when she pulled in. The resulting jolt shot straight up her spine as it flung her forward and back. When the vehicle finally quit rocking, she was surprised the airbag hadn't deployed. She put the vehicle in Park and turned off the flashers and siren before sitting back long enough for her pulse to return to normal. Finally, she put it back in Drive and slowly pressed on the gas pedal.

The cruiser lurched forward and then rocked back again, making it clear that she had bigger problems than letting that speed demon escape. After turning on her emergency blinkers, she got out and used her flashlight to take a close look at the driver's-side wheel. The news was anything but good. Not only was the tire flat, but she was also willing to bet that there was structural damage to the suspension on that corner. Great.

She got back in the vehicle and notified Dispatch that she was out of commission. Next on her list, she called Oscar to see if he could take over patrol an hour earlier than expected. Once she had the rest of her shift covered, she called for a tow. Manny Lopez, owner of the garage in town, answered on the third ring. That was the good news. The bad was that he was finishing up another call, so it could be half an hour before he arrived.

She gave him the location of her vehicle. "I'm parked safely off the highway, so just get here when you can."

With that much settled, she made herself comfortable and considered her options. Manny might be able to give her a ride, but his shop was on the opposite end of town from where she needed to be. If he got another call in the interim, he might not have time to chauffer her around. Should that happen, she supposed she could wake her mother and ask her to come get her. She probably wouldn't mind, but it would mean leaving Gram alone, never the best idea. Unfortunately, her present location was at least two miles from the city center, making it a long walk back to the office. Before she could decide which was the best of two poor options, another vehicle came whizzing by—an all-too-familiar motorcycle.

A few seconds later, it circled around and headed back toward her. The big bike sent up a spray of gravel as its rider pulled off the pavement to stop beside her. She slowly lowered the window and stared at the one man she didn't want to talk to right now. Or ever.

Without saying a word, Titus climbed off his bike and immediately squatted down by the front wheel, using his cell phone's flashlight app to examine the damage. After straightening back up, he rested his hands against the truck and smiled at her.

"Well, Officer Fraser, it looks like you've got a bit of a problem. It's a good thing I happened along right now."

Yeah, it was, not that she would admit it.

"I've already called Manny to come."

"And how soon is he going to get here?"

There was no use in lying about it. She checked her watch. "I'm next in line, so about another fifteen minutes or so."

"Okay, that's one problem taken care of." Titus stepped back. "That leaves the question of how you're going to get back to the police department."

She knew where this was headed, and she didn't like it one bit, even if it beat both of her other two choices. "I could call my mom."

"I'm betting she's already in bed asleep. It would be a shame to wake her."

"That's what I was thinking. I was going to walk."

He turned away to study the road. "Not the smartest thing to do this hour of the night. There aren't many streetlights out this far, making it hard for a passing driver to see you. There's also not much of a shoulder, leaving you walking too close to the road for safety."

His mouth quirked up in a small grin. "And who knows what kind of riffraff would be out at this late hour?"

Even she had to laugh at that. "True enough."

"Tell you what, Officer Fraser. I don't make a habit of picking up hitchhikers, but I'm willing to make an exception in your case. Meanwhile, get whatever you need out of the vehicle before Manny gets here. Once you hand over the keys to him, I'll give you a lift back to town. You can take care of whatever you need to at the station, and then I'll take you home."

"I don't have a helmet to wear. It's the law, you know."

He leaned in close and whispered, "I won't tell if you don't. You can wear mine, and I promise to go slow and drive safely for a change."

When she still hesitated, he opened the door and held out his hand. "Come on, Moira, trust me just this once. You can go back to hating me once I get you back to town."

The only trouble with his offer was the uncomfortable truth that, despite her best efforts, she didn't actually hate him at all.

CHAPTER EIGHT

TITUS FIGURED MOIRA'S stubborn determination to keep him at arm's length was currently at war with her common sense. There was always the possibility that Manny could take her wherever she needed to go. If that happened, there wasn't much Titus could do about it, but evidently he'd made a good argument against her calling her mother. Moira was already busy gathering up everything she needed from the vehicle. Once she had it all together, she reluctantly turned it over to him to stash in his saddlebags just as Manny pulled up.

Titus watched as Moira walked away to talk with Manny. He suspected she was still hoping he would offer to give her a ride. It was a relief when the man shook his head and held out his hand to take her keys. Moira's shoulders slumped just a little in disappointment, but the moment of weakness didn't last long. By the time she headed back in Titus's direction, she was back to being all business.

"Okay, let's go."

Victory was his, but Titus wasn't about to rub it in. Instead, he pulled off his leather jacket and handed it to her. "Put this on."

It was no surprise when she tried to refuse it. "I have a jacket."

"Yours doesn't match my black helmet. I have an image to maintain." He walked behind her and held it up for her to slip on. "Besides, the leather will protect you, not just from the wind but also from a bad case of road rash should something go wrong."

She slid her arms into the sleeves. "And you think that flannel shirt you're sporting would be adequate protection for you?"

He didn't dignify that question with a response. Her safety came first. Rather than argue, he focused on adjusting his helmet to fit her. When he was satisfied, he led her over to the motorcycle. "Have you ever ridden one of these?"

She lifted her chin to give him a superior look. "Yes, I rented a scooter to ride on the beaches over on the coast in Ocean Shores. I didn't crash once."

Now she was just jerking his chain. There was no comparison. He suspected he was sneering a bit when he said, "My Harley would eat those scooters for breakfast."

He liked that she laughed and patted the handlebars on his bike. "Sorry, Harley, no offense intended."

Then she shot him an amused look. "I forgot how sensitive guys are about the size of their motorcycles."

Okay, that was funny. "Tell me, Officer Fraser. When did you get to be such a smart aleck?"

Without waiting for her to answer, he launched into a brief safety speech before climbing on the bike. Then he held out his hand to help her get situated behind him. When she tried to scoot back far enough to avoid touching him, he grabbed both of her hands and tugged them around his waist. "Come on, Moira. I don't have cooties. Hang on tight. It will make it easier for me to balance the bike with an inexperienced rider on the back."

After a second, she leaned in close to his back and tightened her arms around him. He started the engine and carefully guided the bike onto the highway. He maintained a slower than normal speed until she finally relaxed into him. Then he gradually picked up the pace, taking the curves just fast enough to make things a little exciting for both of them.

She tightened her grip a bit, but at least she wasn't screaming for him to slow down. He'd always suspected she was a bit of an adrenaline junkie. Too bad he'd promised to take her directly to the station. Otherwise, he'd be tempted to circle back around to the highway and let her see just how the Harley could eat up the miles.

He wasn't going to do that, though. She didn't need another reason not to trust him. But maybe someday he'd coax her into going on a long-distance ride with him. For now, he'd play the gallant knight and take her to the station. From there, he'd drive her home if she'd let him.

One good deed wouldn't make up for the mistakes of the past, but maybe it was a start.

AN HOUR LATER, he pulled into the driveway at her mother's house. As soon as he did, a light came on up on the second floor. Seconds later, the curtain on that window twitched to the side, and her mother peered out at them. Moira immediately scrambled to get off the bike. As soon as she did, he dismounted as well.

Her eyes widened with what looked surprisingly like panic. "Where do you think you're going?"

"Nowhere, but unless you're going to keep my helmet and jacket, I'd like them back."

She'd already removed the helmet and tossed it to him as the front door opened and her mother stepped out on the porch. Moira all but shoved the jacket at him, too. "Take this and go."

He glanced at Mrs. Fraser and back to Moira. "What's the problem?"

"One of the few rules Mom always insisted on was that I not ride on a motorcycle."

Seriously? "Last I looked, Officer Fraser, you're an adult. Can't you make that decision for yourself?"

"Yes, but I try not to upset my mother any more than I have to. She worries enough because I'm a police officer. She lost a brother in a motorcycle accident when she was a teenager."

Now he felt bad about laughing. Rather

than respond to Moira, he pushed past her to go speak to her mother himself. "Mrs. Fraser, sorry if my motorcycle woke you up. Moira's cruiser broke down out on the highway, and I stopped to see if I could be of help. I swear I drove carefully."

To his surprise, the woman smiled at him. "Thanks for bringing her home, Mr. Kondrat."

His mission accomplished, he winked as he passed Moira on his way back to his bike. "I'm sure I'll see you around, Officer Fraser. Sleep well."

By the time he drove away, Mrs. Fraser had already disappeared back into the house, but Moira paused long enough to watch him drive off. He wanted to think that she was reluctant to see him leave, but it was far more likely that she was wishing he'd disappear from her life just as easily as he disappeared into the night.

It was tempting to head back out to the highway and try to outride his regrets. With some effort, he resisted the urge, knowing that wouldn't be fair to Ned, who was waiting at home for Titus to feed him.

At least when he finally made his way to bed, he could dream about those few minutes when Moira held on tightly and trusted him to get her home safely.

THANKFULLY, IT HADN'T taken Manny long to replace the damaged suspension, so things were back to normal by Monday afternoon. Moira was relieved to have her cruiser back, and she could be back out on patrol.

All things considered, the town had a pretty low crime rate, but there had been another report of a missing cat. Not that anyone had seen anything. From what she could tell, all of the missing animals had simply disappeared. She felt bad for the owners, but there wasn't much the police could do. Heck, even if she spotted an animal out wandering the street, how was she supposed to distinguish it between a pet and a stray unless they were wearing a collar with a tag on it?

Even so, to keep everyone happy, she'd assured the distraught owners that she and the other officers would keep an eye out for anything suspicious as they patrolled their neighborhoods. Who knew how much good it would do, but at least they could say they'd tried. She'd also stopped in to talk to the managers at the feedstore and the market. The good news was that no more pet food had disappeared, something she was happy to put in her report to the council.

She also made a point of driving by Titus's café once or twice a shift, especially at night. She definitely owed the man for giving her a ride home the other night. However that didn't mean she'd give him a free pass on whatever he and that other guy had been up to in the alley when she'd dropped by to give Titus the bottle of wine she'd bought for him.

Doing so made her conscience twinge a bit. He'd been kind to her grandmother and had gone out of his way to reassure her mother after he'd brought Moira home on his motorcycle. He was also friends with her boss, a man she thought was an excellent judge of character. It could be that she was completely off-base in thinking Titus was up to something. Maybe she should do this one last drive-by and call it good.

With that in mind, she turned down the side street that crossed the alley behind the café. Slowing to a crawl, she killed her headlights as she eased up to the intersection. Most nights the only vehicles in the alley were either Titus's Harley or his old pickup truck.

Tonight, she was disappointed to see the van was back. There was no sign of the other guy, but Titus was in the process of locking the doors on the back of the van. She continued to watch as he climbed into the driver's seat and started the engine.

As soon as he drove off, she followed, while maintaining what she hoped was a safe distance. Unfortunately, there weren't many cars on the street this late in the evening, making it almost impossible to hide the fact that she was tailing the man. There were two cars between them, one of them driving at a steady five miles an hour under the posted speed limit. Normally, Moira would have no problem with that, but right now it meant that she was falling farther and farther behind her target. She could have passed the slowpokes, but that would only draw Titus's attention in her direction.

It was a huge relief when both cars turned off at the same cross street. She resisted the urge to gun the engine to close the distance between her and Titus. By this point, it was obvious that he was heading out of town. The stop sign at the end of the block marked the last intersection within the city limits. From there, the road became a two-lane road that led to the state highway that connected two east-west interstates. It would be interesting to learn if Titus was going toward Seattle, Tacoma, or even Spokane on the east side of the state.

How long should she follow him? In another quarter mile, they would cross into the county sheriff's jurisdiction. There was also the fact the Dunbar Police Department was shorthanded right now. If she had actual knowledge that a crime was being committed, it would be one thing. Curiosity wasn't a good enough reason for her to stray so far from her normal territory.

The decision was made for her a few seconds later when she got a call about some minors drinking alcohol and being a nuisance. She listened to what the dispatcher had to say. "Got it. I'll be there in less than five minutes."

She did a U-turn and headed back toward town. She checked her rearview mirror one last time before picking up speed. Unless she was mistaken, Titus had just stuck his hand out of the driver's window long enough to wave goodbye. Torn between laughing and

wanting to punch something—or someone—
she hit the gas and went back to work.

TITUS STARED AT the bag sitting on his desk. He
still owed the goodies it contained to Moira
for the day she'd spent working at the café.
Considering his mood, he should probably
drop them off at her mother's house rather
than delivering them to Moira at the police
station. He hadn't actually appreciated her
tailing him last evening. He glanced down at
Ned, who was curled up in his bed in the far
corner. "So what do you think, dog? Shall we
walk down to the police station and pay an
unscheduled visit to Officer Fraser?"

Ned tipped his head to the side as if actually pondering the wisdom of that idea. He
rose to his feet and gave himself a good shake
before heading out of the office and down
the steps to the kitchen below. "I guess I got
my answer."

At the bottom of the steps, Titus waited
until Gunner finished plating up an order to
catch his attention. "I'm going to deliver this
order of pies. I shouldn't be gone long. Call
if you need me."

"Will do." The other man eyed the bag and

smiled just a little. "Tell Moira hi for me, even though I'd suggest you leave that at the front desk for her. You tend to get all riled up whenever the two of you cross paths. Gotta admit that it makes for an unpleasant work atmosphere."

The man wasn't wrong. Being around Moira did tend to twist Titus up in knots. That didn't mean it was okay to take his bad moods out on his employees. "Like I said, I won't be gone long."

He grabbed Ned's leash on the way out. The dog didn't much like being tethered to Titus as they walked through town, but Ned's size and attitude tended to make people nervous. Or maybe it was Titus himself who was the reason some folks gave him and the dog a wide berth as they walked by. He evidently had that effect on some people. Go figure.

The police department was not far from his café as a crow flies, but he took a more circuitous route than necessary. He did it partly to give Ned a chance to stretch his legs a bit, but mostly he preferred to avoid walking by Bea's bakeshop whenever he could. Her place served as gossip central for the town. He didn't much care what rumors Bea spread about him; it wasn't as if she actually knew much about him or his past. No one in Dunbar did. But that didn't mean he wanted to offer up fodder for the gossip mill if it might link his name to Moira's. She deserved better, especially when she was currently in charge of the police department.

He crossed the street and continued to the next intersection before turning in the direction of the police department. It amused him that Moira had failed miserably to disguise the fact that she was trailing him last night. Thanks to some finely honed survival skills, he almost had a sixth sense that warned him when someone was a little too interested in his business. Besides, that huge black SUV decked out with lights on the roof that she drove everywhere was hardly inconspicuous.

It had been tempting to lead her on a merry chase, but he hadn't wanted to keep the people he was supposed to meet waiting any longer than necessary. They'd already made special arrangements to accommodate his schedule. Still, knowing them, he was pretty sure they would have found it hilarious if he'd pulled up with a suspicious cop hot on his tail. He doubted Moira would've thought it was funny. A smarter man would clear the air and simply tell her what she wanted to know, but it made him mad that she assumed the worst about him.

A soft nudge against his legs accompanied by a low growl broke through Titus's spiraling temper and made him realize that he'd coasted to a stop. He glared down at Ned, who glared right back. "What do you want, dog?"

Ned had about as much patience as Titus did. He expressed his displeasure with a soft growl as he circled Titus's legs, tangling him up in the leash. Before he could get free, Ned lunged forward, nearly tripping Titus in the process. With some fancy stepping, Titus managed to free himself without falling down or dropping the pies. He gave the leash a sharp tug to bring the unruly dog to a quick halt. When Ned begrudgingly sat down, Titus patted him on the head. "Okay, let's try this again."

Ned started forward again, this time carefully matching his pace to Titus's. "Should we see if we can get in the back door of the station or go in the front?"

Like the dog cared about that. Titus headed for the front of the police department. It was a huge disappointment that it was Oscar Lovell standing at the front counter. While he didn't have any problems with Oscar, the man was related to Bea at the bakeshop. The pair appeared to have an ongoing competition over which one learned the juiciest bits of gossip first. Such was life in a small town, something Titus was still getting used to.

Oscar eyed Titus with interest. "Morning, Titus. What can I do for you?"

He tilted the bag so Oscar could see its contents. "I have a delivery for Officer Fraser. Is she in?"

Seeing the disappointment on Oscar's face, Titus bit back a sigh. "I should've thought to bring extras for Dunbar's finest. Dessert is on me the next time you stop at the café."

"That's right decent of you." Oscar jerked his head in the direction of Cade's office. "Moira is working in back. If the door is closed, knock first."

"Thanks, Oscar."

"Before you go, here's a couple of treats for your friend."

He handed the dog biscuits to Titus rather than offering them to Ned himself. Titus didn't blame him for being cautious, even though Ned always behaved himself around people who might feed him. A dog who had spent much of his life living on the street knew better than to ever turn down a free meal.

After tossing the treats to Ned, Titus led him down the hallway to Cade's office. The door was open, but he knocked on the door frame, anyway. When Moira looked up from her computer screen, her expression instantly morphed from welcoming to suspicious.

"Titus."

"Moira."

She rolled her eyes. "Is there something you need? I have work to do."

He held up the bag. "I brought your pies. Sorry it took longer than expected. Things have been a bit busy lately. You know, late-night errands to run. Stuff like that."

She gave him a dark look at that last comment. Clearly, the woman's sense of humor was on hiatus today. "You could've left me a message to pick them up at the café and saved yourself a trip."

"Ned and I were out and about, anyway."

At the mention of his name, Ned circled around to stand next to Moira. To her credit, she positively cooed as she pet him. "You're such a handsome boy, Ned. Are you sure you wouldn't be happier living with someone else? Maybe somebody reputable?"

Titus smirked. "Ned knows when he's got a good thing going. As long as he has a warm place to sleep and a steady supply of food, he's got no room to complain."

He held up the sack again. "So do you want these or not?"

Leaning back in her chair, she pointed at the corner of the desk. "You can set them there."

After putting them down as instructed, Titus tugged on Ned's leash. "Come on, boy. Officer Fraser has work to do, and so do I."

He started out the door, but stopped long enough to add a reminder. "I wouldn't leave the cream pie sitting out for long, but it will be okay for a short time."

She glanced at her computer and back to him. "Thanks, Titus. Gram and my mother will be thrilled. They love your desserts."

"And you?"

"I would think you'd be above fishing for compliments, Titus. But I do, too."

"Good to know. See you later, Moira."

Then he grinned at her. "Or maybe not. I'll be staying in town tonight, so no need for you to cruise by the café this evening to see what I'm up to."

Happy to have had the last word, he whistled as he walked away.

CHAPTER NINE

As it TURNED OUT, Titus hadn't lied about his plans for the previous evening. He had indeed stuck close to home, not that Moira had taken his word for it. She'd still driven by the café three times while she'd been out on patrol. On her last pass, Titus had just locked the café's front door. He had Ned with him, and the pair set off in the direction of their house. She'd slowed to the speed he was walking and rolled down the passenger window.

"You look kind of tired. Do you want a lift home?"

He waved her off. "Thanks, but I need the exercise."

"I wasn't talking to you. I was asking Ned."

That startled a laugh out of the dog's owner. "Funny. I'm sure Ned would love to shed all over your official vehicle, but he needs to burn off some energy. Otherwise, he'll keep me up to all hours."

Moira moved on to another subject. "By the way, both Mom and Gram asked me to thank you again for the pies. Theirs didn't last long. I'm crossing my fingers that they didn't find the last piece of the chocolate that I stashed in the vegetable drawer."

That seemed to please him. "Let me know the next time you want to dust off your waitress uniform and earn a couple more. I make a mean banana-cream, too."

She bet he did. "I'll keep that in mind. Good night, Ned."

Looking back, that conversation had been the high point of last night's shift. A few minutes later, she'd gotten a call about an accident on the edge of town that resulted in two people having to be airlifted to the trauma hospital in Seattle. She'd helped control traffic while the county completed its investigation of the incident and got the two damaged vehicles cleared. By the time she'd gotten home, she'd been too wound up to relax right away. At least her piece of pie had been right where she'd left it. Coupled with a cup of chamomile tea, it had soothed her nerves enough to let her sleep.

Tonight was going better. At least, so far. She decided to take advantage in the lull to return Titus's pie plate and the mini-pie ramekins. She regretted the decision as soon as she turned down the alley behind the café. There was Titus picking up a pair of pet carriers and setting them into the back of the same van he'd been driving two nights before.

When her headlights hit him, he slammed the doors shut and turned around to face her. She continued forward, parking a short distance away but leaving her headlights on to illuminate the scene ahead of her. After putting her vehicle in Park, she got out and started toward Titus.

"Mr. Kondrat, did you just load some cats into that vehicle?"

"And if I did?"

After speaking to several stressed-out pet owners earlier, she was in no mood to play games. "Can you prove that they are yours?"

He patted his pockets and shook his head. "I must have left the paperwork in my other pants."

"Not funny. Several pets have gone missing recently. Two owners received ransom notes and had to pay up to get their animals back."

Now he was looking at her as if she was crazy. "Come on, Moira, what exactly are you accusing me of now? The last time you jumped to the conclusion I was dealing drugs. Now it sounds like you think I'm heading up a cat-rustling gang or something."

Okay, putting it that way did make her feel a bit foolish. She backed off a bit on the attitude and tried again, "Sorry, I didn't mean it to come out that way."

He arched an eyebrow, conveying his disbelief about that. There wasn't much she could say because he wasn't wrong. "Okay, maybe I did, but let me start over. Are those cats strays? We've had reports of pets gone missing, several of them cats. I was hoping maybe those might be two of them."

He opened the back of the van. "I'm sorry to hear that, but these two are a couple of feral kittens."

She peered around him to study them. "What are you going to do with them?"

Titus offered her a teasing smile. "Normally I'd tell you that I'm trying out a new recipe for the café, but I suspect you're not in the mood for tasteless jokes. They're actually the last of a litter that I've been trying to round up for the past month. They're young enough that they might still be able to make a good pet for someone."

She couldn't quite hide her own smile when he poked his fingertip through the door of the closest cage to gently stroke the small calico cat inside. "So I repeat, what are you going to do with them?"

"I'm taking them to a no-kill cat shelter about twenty miles from here. They'll spay or neuter them, give them their shots and then farm them out to someone who fosters kittens. Once they figure out if these fur balls can adjust to living with people, they'll try to place them in a permanent home."

As he spoke, she noticed the stack of bags piled up behind the two cages. She leaned in closer to read the labels. Then, feeling a little slow on the uptake, she finally connected the dots. "You're taking them and that stack of pet food and cat litter to the same shelter."

When he nodded, she sighed. "Just like you and that other guy were doing the last time I saw you loading up this van."

"Yup."

She smacked him on the arm. "Why didn't you just tell me that at the time?"

"Because it made me mad that you immediately jumped to the wrong conclusion. You should have known better."

She felt compelled to state the obvious. "At that point, I didn't know who you were."

"Sure you did, at least on some level."

Moira had no idea what he was talking about. "How do you figure that?"

"Remember the wine you bought me?"

The man was making no sense. "Yeah, what about it?"

"It's the same wine I served when I cooked dinner for you the night before everything went wrong."

Darn it, he was right about that. "But wait, even if that's so, I hadn't given it to you yet. There was no way you knew at that point if I was starting to see through all the changes you've made in your appearance."

He didn't deny it. "That's true, but maybe I wanted to think you'd remember me no matter what happened back then."

Was that regret she heard in his rough voice? "Why would you care?"

He shoved his hands in his hip pockets and leaned against the back of the van. "Because I never forgot you."

"It's been almost ten years, Titus. I won't believe that you haven't dated other women in that time."

At least he didn't deny it. "They don't matter. They never did."

Her brain didn't buy that for one second; her heart desperately wanted it to be true. "I've dated other men."

"I know."

"What's that supposed to mean?" Before he could answer, she retreated a step. "Have you been spying on me?"

Because that would be seriously creepy.

"No, but there's no way a woman as beautiful as you are wouldn't have had your fair share of admirers. The real question is how you've stayed single so long. There had to have been someone along the way who meant more to you than a casual date."

It must have been the night for some honesty. "Yeah, there was one who came close, but he eventually realized he couldn't handle the fact that I was a cop. Seems he wanted someone who worked regular hours and didn't strap on a weapon when she went to work. Between you and him, it shouldn't be surprising that I'm a little gun-shy when it comes to men."

There was more than a hint of anger in Titus's dark eyes as he narrowed the distance between them. "I'm sorry if he hurt you, but I'm not sorry it didn't work out. Partly because it was better to find that out before you married him."

Then he caressed her cheek with his fingertip. "But mostly, for selfish reasons. From the first night we met, I thought you and I were a perfect fit. Nothing has happened to change my mind about that, even if you do have an unfortunate habit of accusing me of all kinds of bad things."

"What do you expect? You let me spend ten years believing you were a convicted felon. It's going to take a while to get used to thinking any differently."

His dark eyes met her gaze head-on. "I'd appreciate if you'd put more effort into doing that."

"Why?"

"Because I'm convinced you might still feel something for me even if you're fighting it." His mouth quirked up in a small smile.

"I'm not a patient man by nature, Moira, but you're worth waiting for."

His words were a balm to her badly bruised ego, but that didn't mean she was eager to take a chance on a man who had already broken her heart once. She pointed at Titus and then back at herself. "The two of us might have fit once. But as I've said before, the man I thought I loved was an illusion. As it turned out, *you* weren't real, not in any meaningful way."

"Oh, I'm real all right, Moira, and so is this."

Then Titus gently wrapped her in his arms and once again kissed her. It was even more potent than the first time as the man gave it his all, doing his best to convince her that she wasn't making the biggest mistake of her life. When he finally released her, he looked a bit stunned. No doubt she did, too. Worse yet, she wanted a lot more of the same. That wasn't going to happen. Not now. Maybe ever.

It was definitely time to retreat before she did something she might regret—like surrender to the same attraction that had cost her so much pain ten years ago. "I'm sorry, but we can't do this again, Titus. You let the lies between us stand for ten years. I won't risk that kind of hurt again."

It took every bit of strength she could muster to walk away.

But she did it, anyway.

CHAPTER TEN

"I RECOGNIZE THAT LOOK."

Titus plunked down Max Volkov's lunch on the table, along with his own. He took his seat and glared at the other man. "What look is that?"

"The same one you and Cade were giving me grief about not so long ago."

As he spoke, Max moved his plate a little closer to his side of the table as if afraid that he might have offended Titus to the point that he'd revoke Max's right to eat in his café. Any other time, Titus would have found that amusing, but he wasn't in the mood at the moment. Evidently sensing his irritation, Max held up his hands. "Sorry, man, I didn't mean to poke the bear. I'll shut up now."

Titus leaned back in his own chair and did his best to chill out. "You can relax, Max. I was thinking about someone else, not you."

"Good to know." Max lowered his hands

and grinned. "So back to the subject at hand. What's Moira done to upset you?"

Titus tightened the grip on the glass of water he'd just picked up, momentarily imagining it was Max's neck. After drawing a slow breath, he gently set the glass down on the table and met his friend's amused gaze. "What makes you think my mood has anything to do with Officer Fraser?"

When Max didn't immediately answer, Titus tried again, this time with a little less growl in his voice. "Seriously, what have you heard?"

"Actually nothing, not even at Bea's bakery. I hung out there yesterday afternoon while I did some online research. Her voice carries, so I heard pretty much everything she said while I was there. Your name didn't come up at all. The only mention of Moira had something to do with missing cats."

Okay, that was good. Titus tried again, "So again, why did you think she's done something to upset me?"

Max's smile was sympathetic. "Because I saw what happened at Cade's wedding reception when she walked in. As soon as you spotted her, you went into full retreat and never came back. If it's any comfort, I'm pretty sure no one else noticed."

Titus wasn't in the habit of pouring out his woes to anyone other than Ned. The dog was a good listener, but not all that great at offering advice. However, this wasn't the best place to spill his guts. He looked around the crowded café to make sure no one was paying undue attention to their conversation while he considered how much to tell Max.

Finally, he said, "This goes no farther than this table. You can't even share it with Rikki. That's more for Moira's sake than mine. They're becoming friends, and it should be Moira's decision how much she shares."

Max frowned. "I don't like keeping secrets from Rikki, but I will this once."

Titus decided to throw the dice and believe Max would keep his promise. "The problem is that the lady and I have a bit of history in the distant past. Let's just say that it had to do with her job in Seattle and leave it at that."

It was hard not to laugh as he watched Max try to process that little bombshell. He started to say something and then shut his mouth before a single word came out. Considering he was both a reporter and a writer, the man no doubt had at least a double dose of both imagination and curiosity. There was no telling what kind of scenario was playing out in his head right now, but Titus bet it was a dandy.

After a bit, Max shot him a wicked grin and waggled his eyebrows. "I'm not going to push for details. However, you should know that I'm pretty sure whatever happened involved handcuffs."

This time Titus gave in to the urge to laugh. "No comment."

"I knew it!"

Then Max mimed zipping his lips as his expression turned serious. "If you need to talk, I'm available. I'll even bring the pizza and beer."

That was decent of him, but Max had other people in his life now whose needs should come first. "You're a newlywed. Doesn't your wife prefer that you stick close to home?"

"Normally, yeah." Max rolled his eyes in exasperation and then pointed his fork at Titus. "But you stepped up to help me protect my family. I'll never forget that."

Titus had been a loner most of his life and sometimes forgot what it was like to have people who actually cared about him. Maybe it was time to share some of his secrets with a friend. "I appreciate the offer, but I'm fine."

It was obvious Max wasn't buying what Titus was selling. Trying to head off any more offers of a shoulder to cry on, Titus pointed toward Max's plate. "Eat. I didn't spend all morning cooking for you to let it go cold."

Max laughed and offered Titus a salute. "Yes, sir. And if I clean my plate, do I get pie?"

"For here or to go?"

Max rubbed his hands together with greedy glee. "Why can't I have it both ways?"

Titus gave Max a considering look. "What would Rikki say about you pigging out on pie twice in one day? Not to mention you didn't even ask for extras to share with her and Carter."

"You know you can be a real jerk sometimes, Titus." He took a big bite of his lasagna and swallowed. "I'll take three of your mini pies to go. I wouldn't want to deny my new wife and son the pleasure of one of your desserts."

It was hard not to be jealous of the man's unabashed happiness about his life these days, not that he didn't deserve it. "You're a good man, Max Volkov, and for that reason they'll be full-size pieces."

MOIRA DEARLY WANTED to rub her temples in case that would ease her headache. Instead, she maintained perfect posture and did her best to keep her temper under lock and key. How did Cade deal with this kind of stuff day in and day out without exploding? It might've been cowardly on her part, but she would have cheerfully slipped out the back of the station if she'd known Otto Klaus was on his way to see her. In her experience, the mayor rarely had an actual opinion of his own. Instead, he chose his course of action based on which way he thought the political winds were blowing.

Right now he was staring at her with what he probably thought was an intimidating glare. Moira wasn't impressed. She'd faced down far too many hard-core criminals to cower in front of a sulky small-town mayor. "Officer Fraser, I remain convinced that you overreacted."

She worked hard to keep her expression neutral. "You've already said that, Mr. Mayor. Twice, in fact. That said, those four teenagers were minors in possession of alcohol, which is illegal. I can print out a copy of the exact law if that would help you better understand the situation. I've already provided copies to both the teenagers involved and their parents."

Otto flushed bright red. "I don't need a copy of the law, Officer Fraser. What I need is for you to realize that you mishandled the situation. It was only a few beers."

"Yes, I'm aware of that. But that doesn't change the fact that the kids were underage, in public and had every intention of driving under the influence. I could have arrested the lot of them or even called the county sheriff to take them into custody. I offered them a fair alternative."

The man simply wouldn't give up. "None of them have any history of prior problems. You should've let them off with a warning. I'm sure they've learned their lesson."

Okay, that did it. She leaned forward, elbows on the desk, and met Otto's gaze directly. "No, they haven't, Mr. Mayor. In fact, they think they're above the law. Two of the boys went so far as to tell me that their football coach wouldn't allow me to force them into taking the alcohol-and-drug counseling program that the high school offers. Something about it interfering with football practice."

"But—"

She cut him off, "That's when I brought them into the station instead of letting them call their parents for a ride."

Otto looked horrified. "You put teenagers in a cell?"

"I told them to wait in there, but I didn't close the door. It's the same thing Chief Peters did the last time something like this happened. When all of the parents arrived, I took them into the conference room to explain the policy that Cade established for first-time offenders. They have to complete the counseling at the high school. Once they do that, their record is cleared. Failure to so means the charges stand. That wouldn't result in jail time, but it will affect their insurance rates."

It would have been nicer if Otto had simply accepted Moira's judgment on the best way to handle the situation, but at least telling him she was following Cade's precedent had calmed him down. "We will revisit this situation with Chief Peters when he gets back, Officer Fraser."

She could only hope that Otto hadn't already tried to call Cade—she wouldn't put it past him. He and several of the council members clearly didn't understand the concept of the police chief being entitled to vacation time.

"Believe me, Mr. Mayor, it's important to impress on kids the dangers of messing with alcohol. I've been a police officer for more than ten years now and have lost count of the number of horrendous accidents I've responded to that were caused by someone driving under the influence. I'd rather those parents be a little mad at me for playing hardball now than to have to knock on their door one night to tell them their son or daughter won't be coming home ever again. No one should have to live with that kind of pain."

Otto swallowed hard and finally nodded. "You're right, of course. I will talk to the counselor at the school to see if they can work their sessions around the football practice schedule."

"That seems fair."

She finally relaxed and sat back. Unfortunately, the mayor wasn't done yet. "One more thing. Have you had any progress in locating the missing pets? My office has gotten multiple calls, and several of the council members are concerned that you might not be putting enough effort into solving the problem."

She could guess which two members he was talking about. "All of us are watching for any suspicious activity while we're out on patrol, Mr. Mayor. We've been in touch with the local shelters and the county animal control people. We've advised the owners to post signs in public areas in case someone has spotted the animals. I've also talked to the county sheriff's office to see if the problem is occurring in other areas besides Dunbar. To date, they haven't received any similar reports. Is there anything else?"

"No, that was all."

He trudged out the door. If she wasn't so mad at him, she would have laughed. She couldn't imagine anyone less suited for public office than Otto Klaus. At least she'd finally convinced him that she'd handled the problem with the teenagers according to department policy. Still, that wouldn't keep him from coming trotting back to whine some more as soon as the parents involved found out that siccing the mayor on her hadn't changed anything.

That was a problem for another day. While she pondered what to do next, she closed her eyes and finally massaged her temples. It might have even helped if she didn't suspect yet another concerned citizen was headed her way. She checked to make sure her ponytail was still high and tight, picked up a pen and tried to look busy as she waited to see who was about to darken her door.

When she finally looked up, she wasn't sure how to react. On the upside, it wasn't the mayor or any of the irate parents. On the downside, it was her grandmother standing there looking a bit confused. Moira was up and moving before she even realized she'd made the decision. "Gram, what are you doing here? Where's Mom?"

Because it was a bad thing if Gram had managed to wander this far from home without her daughter noticing she was gone. Moira needed to call her mom, but not until she got her grandmother settled into a chair. Before she could do that, a second person appeared, this one even more surprising.

Titus stepped across the threshold and gave her grandmother an exasperated look. Ned followed right behind and immediately parked himself next to Gram, who smiled and stroked his head. "Hi, Ned."

Titus looked a bit chagrined when he finally spoke. "Boy, she's quick. Ned found her again, and we were closer to here than the café. TJ stopped us at the front counter because you were meeting with the mayor. When Gram asked to use the restroom, I led her down the hall to the ladies' room. The mayor was just leaving your office, so I ducked back out of sight, figuring you wouldn't want your grandmother's adventures broadcast all over town."

He shot Gram a hard look. "Honestly, I was only out of sight for thirty seconds, but she still managed to get past me. At least she headed here and not out the back door."

Moira appreciated his concern for Gram; she truly did. But knowing Gram had turned into a real escape artist upped the ante on Moira's headache. It was pounding out a harsh rhythm and making her feel queasy. Keeping a hand on the desk to maintain her balance, she made her way back to her chair, reached for her phone and called her mother's number.

While she waited for her to pick up, Moira motioned Titus toward the chair next to Gram's. Her mom answered on the second ring. "Hi, what's up?"

Her mother sounded pretty cheery considering the circumstances. "Mom, do you know where Gram is right now?"

Nothing but silence for several seconds before her mother spoke. "I left her at home with Elsie Redd while I did the grocery shopping. I'm on my way home now. Why?"

"She's sitting in my office. Titus and Ned found her again and brought her here."

Her mother's sigh was heartbreaking. "Elsie's trying to call me. I'd better take it. Then I'll come pick her up."

"No need, Mom. You go on home and deal with the groceries. I have less than an hour until I get off shift today. Gram can keep me company until then while you take a breather."

"Are you sure?"

"She's fine. She's petting her buddy Ned right now."

"I'm sorry, Moira."

"Don't worry about it, Mom."

After she disconnected the call, Moira leaned back in her chair and closed her eyes. It was probably rude to ignore her guests, but she needed a chance to gather her scattered thoughts. A second later, Titus broke the silence. "Have you taken anything for that headache?"

She pried her eyes open to see nothing but concern reflected in his gaze and winced when she made the mistake of shaking her head. "I was about to when Mayor Klaus decided to pay me a visit. If I hadn't had a headache before he showed up, I would have had one by the time he left. I have some acetaminophen in my locker."

"Go take some now. I'll keep an eye on your grandmother."

She didn't even try to argue. "I'll be right back."

"Take your time, Officer Fraser. I'm in no rush to get back to the café, and Ned is happy to keep your grandmother company."

"Thanks, Ned." Moira pushed herself up out of the chair and moved toward the door. "And you, too, Titus. Looks like I owe you another bottle of wine."

He waved off that suggestion. "No, you don't. Besides, I still have the first one. I plan to serve it if you ever let me cook dinner for you."

Even though she suspected she already knew the answer, she had to ask… "You're talking about at the café, right?"

He caught her hand as she passed by. "We both know you're smarter than that, Moira, but we can write your confusion off to the headache. It would be at my place, and I promise to be on my best behavior."

She tugged her hand free and kept walking without responding. It was hard to stay mad at a man who had once again stepped up to make sure her grandmother was safe. That made it all the more important to take her pills and get back to her office. Then she would shoo Titus and Ned back out the door before she did something foolish, like accept his invitation. She had enough to contend with between Gram wandering off, the mayor second-guessing her every decision and the mystery of the missing pets. She couldn't handle another complication in her life, especially one as tempting as Titus Kondrat.

After a quick stop at her locker, she washed

down the pills with a glass of water in the break room, hoping like crazy that they'd kick in fast. Before returning to the office, she grabbed a bottle of water for Gram, a few of the cookies Oscar's wife had baked and a handful of doggy treats for Ned. She also poured two cups of coffee, adding cream and sugar to hers but leaving the one for Titus black, like he preferred. He wasn't the only one who remembered little details like that from their all-too-brief time together in the past.

She distributed the makeshift refreshments and sat back down at her desk. Titus seemed content to sip his coffee in silence. It wasn't long before Gram spoke. She kept her hand resting on Ned as she looked around the office in confusion. "Moira, why am I here?"

No matter how many times it happened, it was excruciating to hear the hint of fear in her grandmother's voice. As usual, Moira tried to reassure Gram with a version of the truth that wouldn't cause her distress. "You went for a walk and ended up close to where I work here at the police department. Ned and Mr. Kondrat thought the three of you would surprise me with a visit."

For a second, she thought her grandmother had accepted the explanation, but then Gram shook her head. "In other words, I got lost again."

She immediately turned to Titus, looking distraught. "I'm so sorry I've caused you so much inconvenience."

When Titus responded to Gram's apology, he did it with such amazing gentleness. "It's no inconvenience to spend time with a beautiful woman, Mrs. Healy."

He winked at Moira as he wrapped Gram's fingers in his and pressed a soft kiss to the back of her hand. "It's even better when I'm enjoying the company of two at the same time."

Gram's cheeks flushed as she giggled like a schoolgirl. "You'd better watch out for this one, Moira. He's a charmer."

That he was, but he was also the most aggravating man Moira had ever met. She offered Ned the last treat she'd brought for him. "Thanks again, Titus. I can take it from here. I'm sure you've got stuff you need to be doing at the café."

At least he took the hint. He finished off his coffee and set the empty mug on the corner of the desk. "Yeah, those pies don't bake themselves."

Before leaving, he smiled at her grandmother one last time. "Take care, Mrs. Healy. Have Moira bring you and your daughter for dinner at the café sometime soon. Ned would be glad to see you, and I'll spring for dessert."

Gram leaned down to give the ever-patient Ned a big hug. "We'll do that."

"Come on, dog. Let's hit the road."

Ned slipped past his owner into the hall. Before following his buddy, Titus pinned Moira with a hard look. "About that dinner I mentioned earlier—you used to love my crème brûlée. To be honest, I understand why you're not interested in picking up where we left off. That doesn't mean we can't be friends."

She listened as the sound of his footsteps faded down the hall toward the front of the station. At least the acetaminophen was taking effect, already reducing the syncopated rhythm that had been playing on repeat in her head. That was the good news. The bad news was that she wasn't the only one who hadn't forgotten a single detail about that dinner ten years ago. The only question was what would happen if she allowed Titus to talk her into a do-over.

Would it be just as special? Even if it was, where would that leave them? They'd been very different people back then, and they'd each gone through a lot of changes in the ensuing years. What was Titus hoping to accomplish? More important, was it worth the risk of having her heart broken again just to see if the spark of attraction they'd enjoyed back then could be rekindled?

Rather than sit there and let her thoughts continue to spin in circles, she decided it wouldn't hurt to knock off a few minutes early. TJ had the front desk covered, and she wasn't on patrol tonight. She logged off the computer and stood up. "Gram, can you please wait here while I check in with my coworker out front? It won't take long, and then I'll drive you home. Mom is expecting us."

Gram slowly nodded. "She's going to be upset, isn't she? I don't mean to cause everyone so much trouble."

There wasn't much Moira could say to that. "Maybe we should pick up a pizza for dinner. Mom is always happier when she doesn't have to cook. We'll order her favorite even though I'm not all that fond of olives. Don't you think that will help her mood?"

Looking more like her old self, Gram grinned. "It couldn't hurt."

CHAPTER ELEVEN

FEELING RESTLESS, Titus paced the length of the living room and back again for the fourth time in the past ten minutes. "Maybe I should've taken Max up on his offer. Some company would be nice about now."

Ned's lip curled up in a canine sneer to express his disdain over his roommate's comment. At least that's how Titus interpreted it. "Sorry, boy. I didn't mean you weren't good company. It's just that Cade, Max and I started hanging out together whenever one of them was having woman troubles. Sad to say, now it's my turn."

The dog stood up long enough to turn around three times before curling up again, this time facing away from Titus. His message was pretty clear. Ned had heard enough whining for the time being. "Dog, normally I would remind you who pays for that expensive kibble you like so much, not to mention all those treats you think you deserve."

Titus kneeled down by Ned's bed and stroked his fur. "However, I think it's time to stop feeling sorry for myself. I'm the one who screwed up everything ten years ago, and I can't blame Moira for not wanting to pick up where we left off."

Ned gave Titus's hand a quick lick, which was as close to sympathy as Titus was probably going to get from anybody tonight. He gave the dog another pat on the head just as the doorbell chimed. "Who could that be?"

As soon as he asked the question, he figured he could guess. Just because he told Max not to bother coming, that didn't mean the man would actually listen. Sure enough, Max was standing on the front porch with a huge pizza box in one hand and a six-pack of a local microbrew in the other. "Surprise!"

It was tempting to grumble a bit, but Titus was actually glad to see him. "Come on in."

Ned indulged in a long stretch before slowly dragging himself out of his bed to join them by the door. Max smiled down at the dog. "Let me set this stuff down, boy, and then I'll give you a proper greeting."

Turning his attention to Titus, he nodded toward the pizza box. "Coffee table or kitchen table?"

Oh, right. Titus should probably make some effort to play host. He pointed toward the couch. "Might as well be comfortable. I'll grab plates and napkins from the kitchen and be right back. Would you like a salad to go with the pizza?"

Max set the pizza on the coffee table and surrendered the six-pack to Titus after removing two for immediate consumption. "Actually, that sounds good if it's not too much trouble."

"It won't take but a minute. Make yourself at home."

On his way out of the room, he called back, "Keep an eye on Ned while I'm gone. After living on the street and dumpster diving for dinner, he's an expert on opening pizza boxes."

In the kitchen, he gathered the ingredients to make a Caesar salad. While he worked, he pondered why Max had landed on his doorstep after they'd agreed that Rikki would prefer her husband of less than three weeks to stay home.

It could simply be Max's reporter's curiosity, but Titus rejected that idea. No, he was pretty sure that Max's presence was motivated by something else. He'd already made it clear that he felt he owed Titus for helping to capture the woman who had terrorized Rikki a few weeks back. But after giving the matter further thought, he rejected that idea, too. Guys might not spend a lot of time spilling their guts to each other, but that didn't mean that kindred spirits didn't recognize one another. Max had come bearing pizza and beer because evidently that's what the male half of the population did when a friend was operating in crisis mode. Not that Titus had ever experienced the phenomenon firsthand before moving to Dunbar.

Before exchanging his badge for an apron, Titus had specialized in undercover work for the DEA. That meant he'd spent more of his time hanging out with lowlifes and criminals than he did his fellow agents. After leaving the agency, he'd bounced around a lot as he worked to polish up his culinary skills. The bottom line was that it had been a long time since he'd stuck around one place long enough to actually make friends.

He only knew the broad strokes of Max's past, but he suspected that something other than needing to do research had driven Max to remain out on the road for weeks at a time. It wasn't until Max had met Rikki Bruce that he found someone who made it worthwhile to give up his wandering ways. The only question was if Titus and Max both having problematic pasts would provide a solid basis for friendship.

Figuring there was only one way to find out, he picked up the salad bowl and plates and headed for the living room. His guest was ensconced at one end of the sofa with Ned stretched out beside him with his head in Max's lap. The pair looked pretty content with the arrangement. Titus set the bowl and plates on the coffee table, then took his own seat on the opposite end of the couch.

Max eyed the salad with interest. "This looks great. A lot fancier than I was expecting."

As usual, Titus didn't know how to respond when someone acted as if the meals he prepared were anything out of the ordinary. "It's just a salad."

It was a relief when Max just laughed and dug right in.

Although Titus had the necessary skills to prepare the kind of expensive meals that were featured in five-star restaurants, it hadn't taken him long to figure out that wasn't the type of cooking he wanted to do for the long-term. Instead, he prided himself on preparing hearty and delicious food for ordinary people, the kind of stuff his grandmother always said would stick to a man's ribs. He liked to think that she would have approved of his career choice.

Nana Kondrat had taken in Titus not long after his mother had remarried, which was less than a year after his father had been killed in combat. His stepfather hadn't much liked Titus from the get-go, mostly because Titus had resented Will's concerted efforts to erase all reminders of his predecessor as soon as he moved in with Titus and his mother. Almost overnight, the pictures of Titus's father had disappeared. Also gone were his medals, as well as the flag that had been presented to his widow and son at the funeral. Starting almost from day one, Titus and Will had faced off on too many occasions to count. Unfortunately for Will, Titus had already been nearly as tall as he was now even though he'd been in his early teens. His stepfather had found it difficult to discipline someone who towered over him.

After one particularly bad confrontation, his mother had once again sided with Will and ordered Titus either to toe the line or leave. To her surprise, he'd gone for curtain number two and walked out. It had taken him three days to hitchhike to where his grandmother lived. He'd be eternally grateful that she hadn't hesitated to open her heart and her home to him.

He credited Nana with saving him.

A movement off to his right dragged Titus out of the past and back to the present. Max had finished off his salad and leaned forward to open the pizza box. "I got the pizza with everything on it. I hope that's okay."

Titus finished up his salad, too. "That's fine. I pretty much eat any kind of pizza."

Max narrowed his eyes. "Even the ones with pineapple on them? Because that might be a deal-breaker on any chance of friendship we might have had."

Titus waggled his hand in the air, indicating he could take it or leave it. "Let's just say I can live without it."

"Fair enough."

Max slid two huge slices of pizza onto each of their plates. "Can Ned have some?"

The dog's ears perked up at the mention of his name. Titus had rules about such things and figured he'd better explain them now if they were going to make a habit of hanging out together. "I'll cut him a few small bites after we're done eating. Otherwise, he'll gulp them right down and then mooch for more."

Max patted his canine companion on the head. "Sorry, boy. I guess we'd better do as the man says."

The dog snorted, his opinion on that concept clear. Then he avidly watched every bite that Max took in a clear attempt to guilt him into bending the rules this one time. Titus hoped Max managed to resist the temptation. Ned already thought he ruled the roost. He wasn't exactly wrong.

It didn't take long to finish off most of the pizza. Titus carried everything back into the kitchen and made good on his promise to give Ned a few bites. After grabbing two more of the beers from the fridge, he rejoined his guest on the sofa.

"Thanks for coming tonight."

"No problem. And just so you know, I'm not neglecting my family by being here. They both had other plans. Some repeat customers checked in to the B and B today who have kids about the same age as Carter. He was having a great time hanging out with them when I left. Rikki was determined to spend the evening getting caught up on paperwork. Between our trips to Portland to pack up my stuff and buying all the things we need to set up my office here, we've let a few things slide."

"Have you decided to sell your place in Portland?"

"Not right away. I've listed it for rent with a property-management company for now." Max stopped talking long enough to shift positions to face Titus more directly. "That's enough about me. Let's get back to the conversation we started at the café today. I believe you mentioned something about you and Moira having a bit of a past when she was a cop in Seattle. I remember asking if it might have involved handcuffs, but in a good way.

I've been on pins and needles all day wondering if I was right about that."

Titus didn't know whether to laugh or punch Max on the arm. Finding it hard to dive right into a long explanation, he stood back up. "Give me a minute."

He headed for the chest of drawers in his bedroom. While he hadn't brought his badge from the café, he did have a couple of other bits and pieces from his past he could share with Max.

When he returned, Ned was back on the couch, too. But this time he was sitting on the center cushion as if waiting to cuddle up by Titus this time. At least Titus hoped that was the dog's intention. He might need that small connection to maintain some semblance of control while he stirred up a whole bunch of bad memories.

With that in mind, he took a big gulp of his beer and set it aside. "I'm betting you've heard a lot of theories and wild guesses about where I came from and what I was doing before I moved here and bought the café."

"A few." Max chuckled a little. "Honestly, I've written down some of the more interesting ones in case I want to try my hand at writing a thriller when I finish the book I'm doing about my great-grandfather. Do you know how many people believe you learned how to cook while behind bars? Seriously, since when does prison cuisine include things like chicken and dumplings and Dutch apple pie?"

Titus was well aware of the whispers that had dogged his footsteps since he'd taken over the café from its previous owner. He found that theory pretty amusing. "For the record, I learned how to make chicken and dumplings from my grandmother. Nana was one heck of a cook."

Another sip of his beer did little to soothe Titus's parched throat, but he wasn't going to stop talking now that he'd finally gotten started on the story. "You already know that Moira was a police officer in Seattle. She and I met at a dance club just by happenstance and really hit it off."

He stared down at the envelope in his lap. "I should've walked away that night. It would have been better for both of us if I had. Instead, I used every excuse I could come up with to see her as often as possible."

He finally dumped the contents out of the envelope and handed the picture on top of the pile to Max. "To be completely accurate, though, the man she met that night was this guy—Ryan Donovan."

Max studied the picture for several seconds and then held it closer to the lamp on the end table to get a better look. "He looks enough like you to be your cousin or maybe even your brother. His nose looks a bit different, and his hair looks lighter. He also has a more slender build."

"Believe it or not, that *is* me. At least it was ten years ago."

He'd expected Max to immediately pounce on the fact that Titus was now living under a different identity. Instead, he pointed at the picture again. "Who is this other guy? He looks familiar."

Someone Titus wished he'd never met. "You might have seen his face on the news. His name is Cian Henshaw. At the time that was taken, he was the second-in-command of a large drug-trafficking ring that operated up and down the West Coast."

Max swallowed hard and looked up in confusion. "I can't help but notice that the two of you look pretty darn chummy in the picture."

"We were. You would've liked him, too.

Cian was charming, funny and generous with his friends." Titus leaned over to point at the watch he'd been wearing when the photo was taken. "He gave me that for my birthday. I looked it up later to see what it cost. Even on sale, the price tag would've topped ten thousand dollars. I don't like thinking about how much product he would've had to move just to pay for it."

The silence stretched out almost to the breaking point before Max finally spoke. "So which one of the alphabet-soup agencies were you working for?"

Titus blinked, both surprised and relieved that Max had immediately jumped to the right conclusion. "I was a DEA agent working undercover."

"And Moira didn't know?"

"No, and I couldn't risk telling her. It nearly killed me to lie to her every minute of every day we spent together. However, I'd been undercover for a year already and couldn't simply walk away because I happened to fall hard and fast for a beautiful woman."

"Did this Henshaw fellow know you were dating a cop?"

"No, so at least I did that much right. I kept

those two parts of my life completely separate. Moira and I had been dating for about two months when the whole thing blew up. The DEA received intel that forced them into moving on Henshaw and his organization hard and fast. I happened to be with him at the time, so I got swept up in the same net as everyone else they could corner. Rather than out me at the scene, the agency tried to protect my cover."

He handed Max another newspaper clipping. "They used some of the local police force to help with the raid that night."

Max's eyes were huge as he studied the picture in the paper. He pointed at one person in particular. "That's you being led away in cuffs."

When Titus nodded, Max moved his fingertip to tap on one of the cops in the background. "And that's Moira."

"Yep. That was the last time I saw her before she moved back here to Dunbar and went to work for Cade."

Max handed back the newspaper and the picture. "Let me see if I've got this straight. You never told Moira you were DEA, and she was there the night you were arrested, along with Henshaw and his associates. You knew she had to be kicking herself for not realizing that she had fallen in love with a criminal, and yet you made no effort to tell her any different."

"Pretty much."

"And somewhere along the way, you decided that the best way to rectify that situation was to buy a café in her hometown and then sit back and wait to see if she would figure out you and Ryan Donovan were one and the same."

By that point, Titus had some serious regrets about consuming so much pizza and beer. "I have to admit that it wasn't my smartest idea. In my defense, my original plan was to let the dust settle after the raid and then tell her the truth. I owed her that much even if she couldn't find it possible to forgive me. Unfortunately, life interfered."

"I take it she knows now."

Titus kept his focus on petting Ned. "She does."

Max gave a long, low whistle. "Am I right in thinking she wasn't happy when you finally told her the truth?"

Titus couldn't help but chuckle. "That's putting it mildly."

Once again, Max surprised him. Instead of laughing, too, he sympathized. "We both know you wouldn't have walked away from her unless you had no choice."

Without waiting for Titus to offer up some excuse, he picked up the picture of Titus standing by Cian again and frowned. "There's got to be more to the story than you've told me so far. What happened to turn the guy in this picture into the man you are now? And I'm not just talking about the surface changes."

Good question. He leaned his head against the back of the couch and closed his eyes. "I said the agency tried to protect my cover—I didn't say they succeeded. The raid that night was only partially effective. They rounded up the majority of the intended targets, but a few managed to avoid capture. Somehow, Cian's younger cousin learned I was a cop. Two weeks after the raid, he and a few of his buddies managed to corner me on the street."

He realized he was rubbing his right knee, once again trying to soothe the still sharp memory of what it felt like to have his kneecap shattered with a tire iron. That had been only one of multiple broken bones he'd suffered that night, but it was the one that continued to play a starring role in his nightmares and flashbacks. He'd still been conscious when it happened. The broken bones in his face had been inflicted after he'd finally passed out.

"I was in the hospital for a month recovering from the multiple surgeries needed to patch me back together. After that, I was transferred to a rehab facility for a long stint while I learned to walk again."

He forced himself to meet Max's gaze. "The gravel in my voice was a by-product of that night in the alley, probably from screaming so much."

At this point, Max was ashen. "I don't know what to say, Titus, other than I'm sorry. Both that it happened and for prying."

"Don't sweat it, Max. It was a long time ago."

Besides, he'd come this far and might as well finish it. "When I was discharged, the agency transferred me to a desk job in an office on the other side of the country. The idea was to see if I would recover to the point where I could return to working out in the field. Looking back, I think I knew I was done wearing a badge before I even got out of rehab, but I gave it a shot and then walked away."

He stroked Ned's fur. "I did a two-year culinary program at the community college and then worked at a long list of restaurants and tried out a variety of styles of cooking. It didn't take long for me to realize that I wouldn't be happy working for anyone else long-term, so I also enrolled in some business classes."

"You were still living on the East Coast?"

"Yep."

Max was looking slightly better and even managed a small smile. "And when you were ready to open your own place, you looked around and decided the only place where you could put your new skills to use was in Dunbar, Washington, population six hundred."

"Pretty much. I figured the people here would appreciate hearty meals and good desserts."

"I don't doubt that's true, but I'm guessing the real reason was you were hoping the one person who mattered to you would move back to her hometown at some point."

"I know that sounds ridiculous, but yeah."

How could Titus explain that it had never seemed like a crazy idea to him? He'd been a man on a mission to set things right, to find some way to turn back the clock to the minute he'd first met Moira and felt something inside him click into place. No one and nothing had ever felt so right since.

But instead of shaking his head in disbelief, Max shook his head with a look of wonder on his face. "All I can say is that was one genius plan. It ranks right up there with me moving to the one town where virtually everyone hated my guts on the off chance I could coax Rikki into giving me the time of day."

Now that was funny. "An interesting parallel I hadn't considered. At least one of us has had his nefarious plan work out."

"Fingers crossed that yours meets with success, too. So what comes next?"

"Good question. Do you want another beer in case a little more alcohol helps inspire an even more genius plan?"

Max held out his empty. "What the heck, it couldn't hurt."

CHAPTER TWELVE

MOIRA'S AFTERNOON HAD started off badly and then gotten worse. For the past fifteen minutes, she'd been on the phone talking to yet another citizen complaining about the failure of the Dunbar police force to locate his missing pampered pet. She wasn't quite clear on what breed Sir Nigel was, but Mr. Humby made it quite clear that the dog had his own bedroom, which was filled with a record number of first-place and best-in-show trophies.

To prove it, the guy had insisted on texting her a series of photos before insinuating that she was cowering in Cade's office when she should be out on the street organizing a manhunt. Or dog hunt. Whatever. He was right about one thing. She needed to hit the road again as soon as she managed to end the call.

Responding to his next threat, she said, "Mr. Humby, there's no need to call city hall."

Mainly because the last thing she needed was for the mayor and his buddies on the council hassling her more than they already were. "I'm sorry, but I've been out on patrol and had only just returned to the office right before you called again. You were already at the top of my list of people to contact."

"I'm not sure I believe you, Officer Fraser," he huffed in disgust. "I had already left several messages, and you hadn't bothered to respond to any of those."

That was because he'd called three times in less than an hour. At the time she'd been responding to a pretty bad fender bender on the other side of town. The man's fourth call came in before she'd even had a chance to sit down.

"I'm sorry about the delay, Mr. Humby, but I was responding to an emergency. Until the ambulance and tow truck arrived, I wasn't in a position to return phone calls. You may choose not to believe me, but the truth is I had just returned to the office five minutes before you called this time."

There was a heavy silence on the other end of the line, followed by a deep sigh that now sounded more resigned than angry. "I apologize, Officer Fraser. I wasn't aware, and I shouldn't have implied that you were shirking your duty."

He'd more than implied it, but she let it go. If she got upset every time someone had questioned a cop's job performance, she would have spent most of the past ten years angry. That would be a waste of both her time and energy. "And as I was about to say, I will be going back out on patrol as soon as I finish returning calls. If I learn anything about Sir Nigel, I will get in touch immediately."

"I would greatly appreciate that. He means everything to me and my wife."

She hesitated before hanging up. "There is one thing you should know. Several other pets have gone missing recently. A couple returned on their own, and I hope Sir Nigel does the same. The thing is, two others came home only after their owners paid a ransom demand. The good news is that both animals had been well-cared for during their absence. There's no way of knowing if this is what happened to your dog. But if you do get demand for payment, please let me know."

There was a quaver in Mr. Humby's voice when he spoke. "We live on a fixed income,

Officer Fraser. I will make some calls to see how much cash I can raise on short notice, but what happens to Sir Nigel if I can't raise the money?"

At least she could reassure him on that score. "That's the odd thing. Each time the ransom demand was less than thirty dollars."

"Seriously? That's almost an insult to a dog like my Nigel. What kind of criminal mastermind are we dealing with here?"

"I have no idea, Mr. Humby. I would ask that you not broadcast what I just told you. I wouldn't want to spook the kidnapper."

"My lips are sealed. I appreciate the warning."

After a brief hesitation, he added, "Stay safe while you're out on patrol, Officer Fraser."

She accepted the peace offering. "Thank you, Mr. Humby. I'll do my best."

The last question after she made her remaining phone calls was if she had time to pick up a meal to go. She'd been about to make her lunch before leaving home when Oscar had called for an assist. She'd been going nonstop since and worked straight through lunch and well into the dinner hour.

To make it all the way to the end of her shift, she definitely needed to refuel. Fast food wasn't her favorite cuisine, but drive-up windows were sure convenient in a pinch. Unfortunately, the closest one was nearly thirty miles away, too far to go when duty required she stick closer to home.

That left only one recourse—calling in an order to the café. She'd love to actually sit down at a table and take the time to enjoy her meal, but she'd have to settle for getting one of Titus's roast-beef sandwiches and a couple of sides to eat as time and duties allowed. She'd do a circuit through town before picking up her meal and parking somewhere while she ate. That way, she could still respond quickly if something came up that required her attention.

It would be nice if one of the staff at the café answered the phone, but with the way her day had gone so far, she had little doubt whom she'd end up talking to. Sure enough, it was Titus's deep rumble that greeted her. "Officer Fraser, I've been thinking about you."

She wasn't about to ask why. "I need to place an order to go."

Maybe Titus picked up on the stress in her voice, because he simply asked, "What would you like?"

She kept it short and sweet. "A roast-beef sandwich with the usual fixings and a side salad. Iced tea to drink. I'll be there in about thirty minutes to pick it up."

"Drive around back and honk. I'll bring it out to you. See you soon."

"Wait, you didn't get my credit-card number."

"Did I ask for it?"

She pinched the bridge of her nose, trying to hold on to her temper. "No, that's why I asked you to wait. We aren't done."

"You're right. In fact, we're far from it."

He managed to thread a whole lot of extra meaning into those few words. When she couldn't do more than sputter in response, he had the nerve to laugh. "Like I said, honk when you get here."

When the line went dead, she slammed her hand down on the table. "Someday that man will go too far."

And if her real fear was that the two of them would never go far enough, well, that was her secret to keep.

TITUS CHECKED THE clock for the umpteenth time. Moira had said she'd be there in thirty minutes, but an hour and a half had passed and still no sign of her. Maybe she'd gotten a call. That would be the most logical reason for the delay, but his gut feeling was that something more was going on. He could only hope that he was wrong, but there was just one way to find out. He called the police station directly. Instead of either Oscar or TJ picking up, it kicked over to Dispatch.

"Nine-one-one, what is your emergency, Titus?"

At least it was someone he knew. "I'm sorry, Jackie, there's no emergency. I was trying to reach one of the officers at the Dunbar Police Department. I didn't realize that the call would get patched through to you if they couldn't answer. My apologies."

"Who were you trying to reach? I can pass along a message if the officer checks in."

"Ask Officer Fraser to give me a call. She has the number."

"Will do."

He hung up and resumed staring out the back window of the café, watching for any sign of her cruiser in the alley. Finally, he grabbed his jacket and whistled for Ned. The last of his staff had left for home already, so there was nothing keeping him there except Moira's order. He grabbed it off the counter in case he found her to save them both a trip back to the café.

"Let's take a look around, Ned."

Hoping to cover more territory in less time, he opened the driver's door on his pickup and stood back to let Ned jump in ahead of him. Once out on the road, he started by circling the center of town and gradually moved outward from there. When he got as far as Shay Barnaby's place with no sign of trouble, his tension eased up, but only a little. Instead of returning to the café, he decided to do another sweep before giving up. It wasn't until he reached the park on the opposite side of town from the tavern that he finally spotted Moira's cruiser.

It was parked at a weird angle, partly on the road and partly on the grass. The lights were flashing on the roof, but there was no one in the vehicle and no sign of Moira in the immediate vicinity. Titus's pulse picked up speed as he considered his options. "Moira would remind me that I'm no longer a cop and that I should call for assistance."

Ned growled, expressing his opinion of that idea. Clearly, he understood the possible urgency of the situation. "I agree, boy. I'll make the call in case she's in trouble, but that's not going to stop me from taking a look around before backup arrives."

He pulled his flashlight out of the glove box before getting out, then held the door open for Ned to join him on the ground. They made their way over to the abandoned cruiser and took a quick look at the interior. No obvious sign of trouble, so he stepped back and studied the surrounding woods. Where could she be?

That's when he noticed Ned had gone on point, sniffing the air like crazy with his ears pricked forward. "Show me, boy."

The dog trotted forward, stopping every so often to get his bearings. They'd gone about a hundred feet into the trees when Titus finally heard Moira's voice. She was too far away for him to make out the words, but her tone was calm and professional. That made him feel marginally better, but he still didn't like the fact that she was alone in the woods with a person or persons unknown.

He dialed TJ's home number, hoping to catch the young officer at his house. "Officer Shaw speaking, Mr. Kondrat. What's wrong?"

"I was out for a drive when I spotted Officer Fraser's cruiser parked near the entrance on the south side of the park. The lights are flashing, but there's no sign of her. My dog took off running into the woods. When I caught up with him, I could hear her talking to somebody. Rather than go charging in, I thought it best to call you first. Stay on the phone while I move closer to see what's going on."

"You should wait for me to arrive. I'm only about a mile from there."

"Sorry, but a lot can happen in the time it would take you to get here. If Moira gets mad, I'll make sure she knows you tried to get me to do the smart thing."

"I'm on my way." There was the sound of a car door opening and closing again. "And for what it's worth, I wouldn't wait, either."

The kid had a good head on his shoulders. No wonder Cade was so high on his newest hire. "When you see the cruiser, head straight into the trees about a hundred feet or so. I could hear her talking at that point. I'm going silent now to see how close I can get without putting her in danger. I don't want to draw unwanted attention in my direction if she's in the middle of something."

"Got it."

Ned stuck close to Titus without having to be told. He kept his nose to the ground, still stopping occasionally to listen before moving on. There wasn't enough moonlight filtering down through the trees to make maneuvering through the woods easy for man or dog. More than once, Titus came close to taking a header when he tripped over a rock or root jutting out of the ground. At least the trees were starting to thin out a bit, as if they were approaching a clearing of some sort.

That made navigating easier, and he could hear Moira speaking more clearly. There was definitely an angry edge in her voice now. That was worrisome enough, but it was the other person involved in the conversation who set Titus's teeth on edge. Ned started to growl deep in his chest, so Titus wasn't the only one reacting badly to whatever was going down just ahead. Unless he was mistaken, Moira was facing off against the same guy she'd tangled with outside Shay Barnaby's place last week. Jimmy something, not that his name was important at the moment. What had that jerk done now?

It was time to give TJ an update before moving closer to the confrontation. Titus moved back farther into the trees before speaking. "Sounds like Moira is dealing with that Jimmy guy who spent a couple of nights as a guest of the county jail. I'm almost within sight of them. Near as I can tell, they're talking for now. I'll let you know if that changes."

"Hang back if you can. I can see Moira's vehicle, so I should catch up with you shortly."

"I'm going silent again."

Without waiting for a response, Titus moved back, closer to where Moira and Jimmy were still facing off. This time he positioned himself where he was slightly behind Jimmy's position. If it all went sideways, he'd have a better shot of reaching Jimmy before the man would even see Titus coming. Easing forward and a few more steps to the right, he had an unobstructed view of the situation. Nothing about it made him happy.

Moira was sporting her best cop face as she stared down her opponent. Jimmy was perched on top of a picnic table as he glared right back at Moira. It might have been more impressive if he wasn't swaying back and forth and having trouble staying upright. The scattering of empty beer cans on the table and the surrounding ground made it even more obvious the man had been doing some serious drinking.

For the moment, the conversation between the two had apparently ground to a complete halt. Moira relaxed her stance as if she had all day—well, actually, all night—to deal with the situation. Her calm silence wasn't having the desired effect on Jimmy, though. Titus braced himself for action as the man became more agitated as the seconds ticked by. When Jimmy finished off the beer in his hand, he tossed the can aside and reached for another.

"You have no right to kick me out of the park, Officer. I'm a citizen, and I pay taxes."

He paused to belch loudly before continuing his tirade. "At least I did pay taxes when I still had a job."

He pointed a shaky finger in Moira's direction. "And it's your stupid fault that I don't have one anymore. My boss didn't much appreciate me not showing up for work the next morning without calling in. Funny how the county jail doesn't care about such things. They eventually let me call my mother to hire an attorney to get me out of there, but I couldn't call anyone else."

"I'm sorry to hear about your job, Jimmy, but I don't see how that was my fault. Maybe if you can lay off the beer, he'll reconsider. If you want to get into a program, I can put you in touch with some people."

He popped the top on his beer and downed at least half the can without even pausing to draw a breath. After setting it aside, he went back to pointing. "For your information, Officer, what I drink on my own time is not his business. Yours, either. If you'd gotten my keys back from Shay Barnaby like I told you to, none of this would've happened. I wasn't drunk and disorderly—I was hanging out with my friends. We didn't cause no trouble, leastwise not until you showed up and started throwing your weight around. You even got my friends to turn on me. Toby hung up on me when I tried to call him."

His head wobbled as he looked around the clearing, as if he expected to see his former buddy standing around. "The big coward let your cop friend drive him home like he was some kid too young to have a drivers' license. Now that I think about it, I'm madder at him than I am at you."

Moira finally spoke again. "I'm sorry you're upset, Jimmy, but I still have to ask you to leave the park. It closes at sundown, which was a while ago. If you come along peacefully, I won't write you a ticket this time."

As long as Jimmy remained seated, Titus would continue to hold his current position. TJ should be arriving any second now and could step in if Moira needed support. With luck, Titus and Ned could then melt back into the trees without getting involved. Not that he wasn't fighting a strong urge to go charging to the rescue, anyway, even though Moira had the matter well in hand. Unless that changed, he'd stay right where he was.

To help keep himself grounded, he stroked Ned's fur, taking comfort from the dog's warm presence at his feet. A few seconds later, a twig snapped, ratcheting up Titus's already high stress level. The noise came from somewhere behind his current position. Ned stood up, on full alert.

"It's me, Mr. Kondrat. Can you ask your dog to stand down?"

"Sit, Ned. Officer Shaw is Moira's friend."

After giving the air a good sniff, Ned turned his attention back to the clearing and sat down, leaning into Titus's right leg. TJ sidled up to stand next to Titus on the other side. "Sitrep?"

"The man's drunk and upset. She's trying to talk him down. I've only heard part of the conversation, but he blames her that he lost his job while he was locked up. Something about the county jail not letting him call in sick to work or something. Moira just reminded him that the park closes at sundown and that he needs to leave. She even offered not to write him a ticket if he cooperates."

TJ shook his head. "Fat chance of that happening. I've dealt with Jimmy a time or two myself. Once he digs in his heels, he never backs down."

The second Moira shifted slightly, Titus knew she'd run out of patience. "Mr. Hudson, we've been out here long enough. I have to get back on patrol, and I can't do that until I know you've made it home safely."

The man jerked as if her words had hit a raw nerve. "And where would that be? Toby kicked me out after I punched him for letting me go to jail by myself. My mother paid the attorney to get me sprung, but she said until I got sober I wasn't welcome at her house. With no paycheck coming in, I can't afford a motel."

He shifted forward, sliding down onto the seat of the picnic table and planting his feet on the ground. "I'm not going anywhere because I ain't got nowhere else to go."

Then he sneered as he looked at her. "And I'm betting you can't make me this time. I still haven't figured out who helped you take me down that night outside of the bar. Ain't no woman alive who could do that without help. Was it that other cop or did that Kondrat guy and his dog ambush me? Everybody knows that guy did hard time. I should sue him for attacking me for no reason. His dog, too. Then I'd have money."

Under other circumstances, that last bit would have been funny. Right now, though,

TJ was giving Titus a dark look. "You and the dog were there that night? I didn't see you."

"Ned and I were out for a walk. Ned didn't like the way those guys were talking to Moira and growled. He was on his leash the whole time and didn't go anywhere near them. From what I could see, she had things handled and backup was on the way. You must have arrived right after we left."

Actually, he knew exactly when TJ pulled up because he was watching from the shadows between two nearby buildings. Moira had been mad enough that Titus had been there at all. If her coworker had known he had almost waded in and knocked heads to protect her, she would have tossed him in the slammer right next to Jimmy.

All of which meant it was probably time for him to make a strategic retreat again. Once he was back at the road, he'd text Moira and tell her that he'd put her dinner in her SUV. "Now that you're here, Ned and I will head home."

But before he'd taken a single step, Jimmy went into launch mode. Titus let go of Ned's leash, ready to do battle.

CHAPTER THIRTEEN

MOIRA KNEW BETTER than to take her eyes off the target, but that didn't mean she wasn't aware that she and Jimmy were no longer alone. A few seconds ago, a movement off to her right had caught her attention. A man was now standing in the deep shadows under the trees, watching her and Jimmy, and he wasn't alone. The ambient light might have been too dim to make out his features, but she knew exactly who was standing watch—Titus and Ned.

A slow burn of frustration flowed through Moira's veins, but she made every effort to hide it. Darn the man, she'd warned him once already not to follow her around, even if this time she was almost glad he was there. With luck, she wouldn't need his help, but there was no telling how this was going to play out. She pulled out her cell phone to call TJ and ask him to come running. Before she could, he stepped into sight. Since she hadn't called him, it only made sense that Titus had done the honors. At least he'd thought that far ahead.

That didn't mean she was going to stand here all night waiting for Jimmy to either pass out or go on the attack. At the rate he was downing beers, it could go either way. He finished off the one he'd just opened and tossed the empty down with the others. He reached into the cardboard carton sitting next to him on the table only to realize it was empty. Frowning, he looked around, as if wondering who had stolen his last beer.

"Jimmy, let me give you a ride..."

She immediately regretted making the offer again, because where could she take him? If his roommate had kicked him out and his mother wouldn't let him come home, where else was there? The only possibility she could think of was sure to light his already short fuse, but something had to change. They couldn't stay out here in the woods all night. "Jimmy, if you need a place to sleep, I can let you use the cot in the cell at the police department."

He came up off the picnic table in a blur

of motion, his fists clenched as he bellowed, "I'm not going back to jail. That's why I'm in this mess in the first place."

TJ darted out of the shadows with Titus right on his heels. Moira veered in his direction, determined to prevent him from making a huge mistake. "Stop, Titus! TJ and I will handle Jimmy."

Somehow.

She moved closer to Jimmy, aiming for calm but not sure how successful she was being as she tried again, "I didn't say you were under arrest, Jimmy. I'm simply offering you a warm place to stay tonight. The cot might not be all that comfortable, but it has to beat sleeping on a picnic table. If you can think of someplace better, I'm open to suggestions."

His face flushed red as he sneered, "I have all kinds of suggestions for you, lady, and none of them involve me spending another night in jail."

He staggered two steps forward and almost tripped. When he caught his balance, he spun around as if trying to figure out if someone had pushed him. The quick move only succeeded in sending him stumbling back toward the picnic table. Moira held her ground, waiting to see what he'd do next. At least Titus and the dog had retreated to the edge of the trees, leaving her and TJ to deal with the real problem.

One way or the other, it was time to bring this little party to a close before Jimmy did something that set Titus off again. Like she'd told him last time, she wouldn't put up with vigilante justice. By that point, Jimmy had now regained his balance, if not his composure. He glared at TJ. "Where'd you come from?"

Without giving him a chance to respond, Jimmy focused on Titus. "What are you doing here? I told you and that dog the last time to stay out of my business."

He shook his fist in Titus's direction. "It's bad enough I don't have a job or a roof over my head. But thanks to you and your buddy Barnaby, I can't even get a hot meal in town. I've been living on gas-station food and cheap beer."

Continuing his tirade, he spun back toward Moira. "I was out here minding my own business when that lady cop showed up to hassle me. That ain't right. I wasn't bothering no-body. Not this time."

At least Titus kept his mouth shut this time while TJ peeled off to head in Moira's direction. He positioned himself near enough for her to hear him whisper, "How do you want to play this?"

"Best case, I want to get Jimmy out of here without the situation getting any worse."

She glanced toward Titus, who was lean-ing against a handy tree with Ned by his side. He'd been talking to the dog but turned in her direction as if he'd sensed her watching him. Something occurred to her. Every time there was a problem of some kind, Titus's imme-diate response was to bring food. He'd done it back when her boss had tossed his now wife in jail overnight for obstructing a police investigation. He'd also offered her grand-mother pie and tea when he'd found her out on the street. More recently, he'd brought sand-wiches and treats to the police station. Maybe she could take advantage of his generosity one more time.

She took a step closer to Jimmy to keep his focus on her. "Jimmy, I'm going to make you a onetime offer. If you agree to come along to the station peacefully, I'm going to ask Titus to bring you one of those hot meals you mentioned. You'll feel better once you've eaten, and you can get a good night's sleep on the cot. Come tomorrow, we'll figure out what can be done about your other problems. How does that sound?"

It was a relief that Jimmy didn't reject the idea out of hand. He squinted at Titus as if trying to decide if the offer was on the up-and-up. "You got any of the meat loaf special left? It's my favorite."

Titus didn't hesitate. "I believe I do. I can heat up a couple of slices along with all the fixings."

He moved back into the clearing while making sure he didn't get between her and Jimmy. "Come to think of it, I also have that bread pudding you had the last time you came in. While Officer Fraser gets you settled in at the station, I'll go back to the café to fix your dinner."

Moira suspected she wasn't the only one holding her breath as they waited to see what Jimmy decided. Finally, he nodded. "I'll go with her."

Then he looked down at the cans scattered

on the ground. "First, I should pack up all of those. Shouldn't leave a mess in the park. Bad example for the kids."

He nearly toppled over when he bent down to pick up the closest can. In a quick move, TJ caught him before he hit the ground. "Easy there, Jimmy. Why don't you sit for a spell?"

Moira positioned herself on his other side, careful not to crowd the man now that he was making some effort to cooperate.

Titus bent down to pick up the closest can from the ground. "Jimmy, would you hold Ned's leash for me while I pick up the cans for you? It won't take but a minute."

Jimmy finally sat down and latched on to Ned's leash. Titus made quick work of dumping all of the empties back into the carton. When he finished, he took back Ned's leash. "I'll head to the café. It won't take me long."

Meanwhile, TJ gave Jimmy a helping hand off the bench. "Come on, Jimmy. Let's head back out to where Officer Fraser parked her vehicle. It's not far."

Moira waited until the two men disappeared into the woods before she confronted Titus. She also needed the time to figure out what she actually wanted to say to him.

Maybe she'd start with the basics and go from there. "I warned you about following me."

"You did."

"And yet here you are."

Instead of being properly cowed by her disapproval, he gave her an aw-shucks grin. "You didn't pick up your dinner, and I hate to have good food go to waste. When it was time to lock up and go home, I figured I'd take your meal with me in case I happened to see you while I was out and about."

Oh, brother. "Right, and you just happened to be driving by the park, which is in the complete opposite direction from your house."

He shrugged. "What can I say? I have a poor sense of direction sometimes."

She was fighting a losing battle and knew it. "You called TJ."

"I did. I was only going to hang around until he arrived. If Jimmy hadn't started getting all worked up, you would've never known I was even here." His teeth gleamed in the moonlight when he smiled again. "Former undercover cops have some serious skills when it comes to skulking around in the shadows, you know."

Fighting the urge to grin right back at him,

she shook her head sadly. "Sorry, big guy, but I've got news for you. Those skills you're so proud of are seriously rusty. I saw you approach the first time and then retreat. I'm guessing that's when you called TJ, and then you came back again."

"Well, that is disappointing. At least give me credit for not charging to the rescue...not that you needed rescuing. I learned from my mistakes."

Maybe he had.

He stared down at her, his dark gaze intense. "I wish the mayor and the council had been here to see you in action. You were amazing."

His assessment meant a lot, but she was glad it was dark out so he couldn't see her blush. Meanwhile, it was time for her to also give credit where credit was due. "I know I didn't give you much choice, Titus, but I appreciate what you're doing for Jimmy. It likely made the difference in getting him to come along peacefully. He still would've ended up sleeping in the cell, but with the door locked. Not only would charging him involve a lot of paperwork for me, but it wouldn't help his current situation at all."

"It's just some leftover meat loaf." As usual, Titus looked uncomfortable with her grati- tude and immediately changed the subject. "Speaking of that. I still have your sandwich and salad, but they're pretty old by now. We'd better catch up with TJ so the two of you can get Jimmy settled at the station. I'll fix enough food for all three of you."

Not only was the man a natural-born pro- tector, but he also had such a generous heart. She wasn't wrong in believing that the guy she'd fallen in love with ten years ago hadn't been real, but her heart badly wanted to be- lieve the man standing in front of her was. After taking a quick peek to make sure that TJ and his companion were out of sight, she caught Titus's head with her hands and tilted his head to the perfect angle for a quick kiss. It was unprofessional, not the right time and absolutely perfect.

He frowned down at her. "Not that I'm complaining, but what was that for?"

"You're a smart man. Figure it out for your- self."

They started walking, and he snapped his fingers as if the answer had just come to him. Leaning in close, he whispered, "I've got it.

You're hoping I have enough bread pudding to go around."

She couldn't help but laugh, which felt pretty good. It had been a long day and a tough one at that. An hour ago, all she'd wanted was for it to end, so she could crawl into bed and pull the covers over her head. But right now, walking through the woods in the darkness with Titus Kondrat, well, there was nowhere else she wanted to be.

"YOU LOOK LIKE HECK."

Titus dropped into the seat across from Max. "Thanks. Good morning to you, too. If you're going to be a jerk, maybe you should take your breakfast and go straight to…someplace else. The door's back that way."

Rather than being offended by Titus's ill temper, Max now looked concerned. "Seriously, is everything okay?"

Needing the energy boost that caffeine would give him, he waited to answer Max's question until he'd gulped down almost half a cup of the miracle cure that was dark roast. Setting his mug back down on the table, he sighed. "Yeah, despite appearances, I'm fine.

Mostly, anyway. It's been a while since I pulled an all-nighter."

Max's eyes flared wide in surprise. "Tell me you were doing something fun that involved our favorite lady cop."

Not a question that Titus wanted to answer in public, but at least Max had the good sense to keep his voice down. "It did involve Officer Fraser, but unfortunately Officer Shaw was there as well. We…well, actually *they* were dealing with a situation. My contribution was limited to meat loaf."

That was as much as he wanted to say on that subject, so he gave Max's plate a pointed look. His friend took the hint. "Fine, I'll eat."

Rita swung by to top off his coffee. To Titus's surprise, she also set a plate in front of him that was piled high with ham and cheddar scrambled eggs with a side of hash browns. "What's this for?"

"It's for you to eat. Gunner pointed out that you're running on empty, which we all know makes you a bit…well, let's just say, temperamental. We've got everything covered right now, so take your time and relax."

He arched an eyebrow. "Remind me, who's the boss around here?"

Rather than cower at the growled question, she laughed at him. "You are, sir. That means it's the job of us minions to see to your every need."

She pointed at the plate. "And right now, you need to fuel up."

Turning her smile in Max's direction, she asked, "Mr. Volkov, can I get you anything else?"

"Nope, I'm good. I'll make sure he cleans his plate."

Great, everyone was a comedian today. "*He's* sitting right here and can decide for himself how much he wants to eat or even if he wants to eat at all."

Titus glared first at Max and then at Rita. Judging by how she kept laughing as she walked away, he needed to work on his intimidation skills. It didn't help that Max wasn't making any effort to hide his amusement as he stuffed his face with the spinach-and-mushroom omelet he'd ordered.

What made matters worse was knowing that Gunner and Rita were right. Drinking all that strong coffee on an empty stomach hadn't been the smartest thing to do. Neither was shoving the food in his mouth as fast as he could. With some effort, he forced himself to slow down and actually enjoy his meal. When he'd finished off the eggs and most of the hash browns, he set down his fork and pushed his plate over to the side of the table.

Max had finished his meal as well, which left him free to start pestering Titus with more questions. "So Moira was acting in her official capacity during your late-night encounter with her."

Titus set down his cup without taking a drink. "You're not going to be happy until you wheedle every detail out of me."

Looking a bit insulted, Max said, "I'll have you know that I do not wheedle. I'm a highly trained reporter. I investigate."

"Right now, you're a highly trained pain in my backside."

Max fell silent for several seconds. "Fine. I'll back off for now, but I'm available if you need to talk about anything."

Once again, Titus wasn't sure how to deal with having so many people who seemingly cared about his personal well-being. It wasn't that he didn't believe them. What he didn't understand was why they would care so much. Max already knew more about Titus's past than anyone else did…including Moira. That wasn't right, and he'd have to change that if he ever hoped to get past the defenses she rebuilt every time he thought they'd made some progress.

It wasn't fair to treat Max like a guinea pig, but Titus had to start somewhere.

"She called and ordered a dinner to go last evening. She was supposed to pick it up thirty minutes later, but she never showed. She warned me once not to interfere with her job, but I got worried. After I locked up the café, I went looking for her. I eventually found her out in the park dealing with a situation."

"So despite her telling you not to follow her around while Cade is gone, you did it, anyway."

"Pretty much. I can't remember if I told you about the night that her vehicle broke down, and I gave her a ride back to the office and then home. I was worried something like that had happened again, especially when I spotted her cruiser at a weird angle by the park with the lights flashing."

Come to think of it, she never explained why she'd left it that way. Not that it mattered right now. "Anyway, I took it to mean that she'd spotted something—or someone—and took off running. Ned and I went through the woods to see what was going on, and I called Officer Shaw in case she might need his help."

"Was she mad about you showing up?"

"Put it this way, she wasn't exactly thrilled, but it ended on a good note." He was thinking about the way she'd kissed him afterward, not that he was going to share that private moment with Max. "Anyway, I ended up coming back here to fix a meal for her, TJ and someone else, who shall remain nameless. By the time I finally got home, I couldn't unwind enough to go to sleep."

"How much rest did you actually get?"

"Not enough."

Or any at all, actually. He'd ended up going out walking until it was time to show up for work. It wouldn't be the first time that he'd had to go without sleep and still function. That's why he'd been guzzling extra strong coffee since he'd arrived at the café to fix the breakfasts he'd promised to Jimmy and whoever had ended up babysitting him last night. Luckily, Oscar Lovell happened to stop in to buy a breakfast sandwich to go. Since he was about to go on duty, Titus had asked him to deliver the meals instead of taking them over himself.

Meanwhile, Max was talking. "Anything I can do to help? Rikki isn't expecting me back at the B and B until this afternoon. I can wash dishes, seat customers—whatever you think I can handle."

"I appreciate the offer, but we're good."

"Just let me know if that changes." Then Max looked past him toward the door. "Wow, Officer Fraser looks like she's not doing much better than you are this morning."

Titus risked a quick glance in her direction. Had Moira been the one who had ended up watching over Jimmy? She and TJ had still been arguing over who should get stuck spending the night at the police station when Titus had left. Or maybe something else had happened that had required her attention. There was always the possibility that Mrs. Leary had wandered off again. He hoped not, for her sake, as well as for Moira's and her mother's.

To his surprise, Moira didn't wait for Rita to direct her to a table. Instead, she looked around the room and then made a beeline in his direction. Max immediately started to stand up. "I should be going."

He probably thought Titus would prefer to be alone with Moira. Any other time, that might've been true, but right now he would rather have the other man there to provide a buffer between him and Moira. "Stay where you are. I'm not sure what's happened now, but I might need you to referee."

Max settled back into his seat. "If you're sure…"

For the first time all morning, Titus felt like smiling. "When it comes to that particular woman, I'm never sure about anything."

CHAPTER FOURTEEN

MOIRA HAD TO be out of her mind, but right now she didn't care. There was a perfectly good empty table on the near side of the café. She could sit there, order a cup of coffee with some kind of pastry and enjoy a few minutes of relative peace before moving on to the next stop on her lengthy list of errands. She could've also done the same thing at Bea O'Malley's bakery a few doors down and not run the risk of running into Titus Kondrat.

Instead, here she found herself bypassing the empty table and heading straight for the man himself. The department owed him for the meals he'd so generously donated to the cause last night. As the person temporarily in charge, it was her duty to officially thank him. She'd already tried to pay for the food, but he'd refused to take a dime from her even when she'd assured him that she could put it on her expense account.

That much was true even though there was no guarantee that she'd actually get reimbursed. She wasn't sure if Cade could okay providing meals for someone who wasn't exactly a prisoner since no actual charges had been filed. She'd let Jimmy off with a warning, making him more of a guest than an actual prisoner.

She forced herself to maintain a steady pace across the short distance to where Titus was sitting with Max Volkov. It would be better if she didn't discuss police business in front of a civilian other than Titus, but right now she couldn't muster enough energy to care. By the time she reached the table, Titus was up and pulling out a chair for her. As much as she normally appreciated such courtesy, it would've been better if his actions hadn't drawn so much attention in their direction.

Rather than comment on it, she did her best to act as if having the most mysterious man in town demonstrating some good old-fashioned manners was something that happened every day. When she was settled, Titus walked away after saying he'd be right back. That left her sitting with Max, someone she still didn't know all that well.

He must have picked up on her unease. After a brief hesitation, he quietly spoke. "Titus was just telling me that it was a late night for him and that it probably was for you as well. He didn't share much in the way of details other than he did some cooking to help you out last night. From the way he's been swilling down coffee, it's obvious he's dragging a bit this morning."

So she hadn't been imagining the exhaustion she thought she'd seen in Titus's eyes. She hadn't gotten much sleep herself, but that was because she spent the night sitting at Cade's desk and wading through paperwork until all hours. Ordinarily, she would've caught some shut-eye on the cot in the break room, but Jimmy hadn't actually been locked up. Knowing that he could go wandering whenever the mood struck, she hadn't been willing to take that risk.

At least she was scheduled to be off after TJ came in at ten. Her original plan had been to go home and crash for a few hours, but then an unexpected phone call had put that idea to rest. As soon as Titus settled in one spot long enough for her to thank him, she would focus her sleep-deprived brain on dealing with the new problem that had been dumped in her lap.

He reappeared carrying a tray containing a pot of tea and a stack of small plates. The top one held three huge cinnamon rolls. He set the tea and a mug in front of Moira and then slid one of the rolls onto each of the two extra plates, keeping the third one for himself. Finally, he handed out the three forks he'd stuck in his shirt pocket.

He got rid of the tray while she eyed the gooey goodness. When he returned, she pointed out the obvious. "You've already fed me once this morning."

He picked up his fork and dug right in. "Consider it dessert."

Okay, that was funny. "I wasn't aware that people were in the habit of eating dessert with breakfast."

Not that it was going to stop her. She took a bite and nearly moaned as the flavor of yeast laced with cinnamon and maybe a bit of cloves hit her tongue. "Did you make these or did Gunner?"

Titus gave her a suspicious look. "Does it matter?"

"Of course, it matters." She scooped up a bit of the icing and licked it off her finger. "I wouldn't want to kidnap the wrong guy and force him to become my pastry slave for life." Max almost choked on the bite he'd just taken as Titus gave her a considering look. When he didn't immediately answer, she asked again, "Seems like an easy question. Was it you or Gunner?"

His voice was a deep rumble when he finally responded. "Considering your nefarious plans, I'm tempted to lie. However, since I told you enough lies in the past, I'm not going to now. Gunner produced this batch, but I taught him how to make them and let him use my recipe."

"Well, that does pose a problem, doesn't it?" She smiled just a little. "Which one of you makes the pies? Oh, and the chicken and dumplings?"

He nudged her with his shoulder. "That's all me."

She nudged him back. "Okay, then it's settled. I won't be kidnapping Gunner."

He swiped his hand across his forehead and grinned at Max. "Whew, that was a close one.

I almost lost the best cook I've ever worked with."

Max pointed his fork at Titus. "That's great for you two—you get to keep your cook while she gets pastries and dumplings for life. What about the rest of us? Are we supposed to go without your pies while you spend all your time baking for her?"

Before either of them could answer, he aimed the tines in her direction. "And you, Officer Fraser, you're sworn to protect and serve. How can you call it *serving* if you keep all the pie for yourself? Sounds like some serious dereliction of duty to me."

Boy, she'd needed this bit of silliness. Playing along, she raised her hands in surrender. "You're right, Mr. Volkov. It would be unbelievably selfish of me to keep Chef Kondrat's skills all to myself."

"Don't I have a say in this?"

As he spoke, Titus gave her one of those looks that made her wish they were someplace a lot more private, although it was probably better that they weren't. "Nope. It's your civic duty as owner of the only full-service eatery in the entire town."

Then she leaned in closer and whispered,

"But if you want to bake me a chocolate-cream pie now and then, I won't tell anyone."

"It's a deal."

She liked that she'd made him smile and that he wasn't looking quite so tired now. The interaction felt comfortable and a little bit familiar. More like the easy relationship they'd had when they'd first met than the sometimes awkward, sometimes infuriating encounters they'd had since she'd learned the truth about who he was. Titus had definitely changed in the ten years since they'd been together in ways that went far deeper than the tattoos that were so much a part of his persona now. However, more and more often she caught a glimpse of the man she'd known and liked so much back then. He'd been more…lighthearted, she supposed was the best description. She suspected that was true for her as well.

Unfortunately, it was time to get down to business and finish her cinnamon roll. "I can't stay long. I wanted to thank you again for helping out last night and feeding everybody this morning. We all appreciated it."

He acknowledged her gratitude with a bare

hint of a nod. "How was the unnamed party doing this morning?"

Again, she probably shouldn't respond in front of Max, but it wasn't as if anything ever remained secret for long in Dunbar. "Having two square meals and a decent night's sleep seems to have made a big difference. We discussed some options, and I'm hopeful he might start making better decisions."

Titus looked pleased by that. "Good to hear."

"Yeah, I took a chance and talked to his employer myself. Turns out our guy is only suspended. If he gets some help, his job will be waiting for him. His mom also said he can return home until he can get things arranged."

"Boy, you have been busy this morning. I hope you-know-who appreciates it."

"Me, too." She checked the time. "Oops, I'd better be going."

When she started to stand, he stopped her. "Shouldn't you be off duty by now?"

"Yeah, but something's come up." She relaxed back in her chair again. "I promised to help find someone who can umpire a couple of little-kid baseball games later today. It's the local fall ball league. Evidently, Cade had volunteered to be a substitute ump when the regular guy can't make it. Since Cade's still on his honeymoon, that leaves them short-handed. Thomas Kline, the guy in charge, has called everyone he could think of with no luck. I would do it myself, but I don't know the finer points of baseball. I played volley-ball and soccer when I was in school."

Titus went perfectly still, then blurted, "If they're that desperate, I could do it. I played center field from junior high school all the way through college. The rules can't have changed all that much."

She didn't know which one of the three people at the table were the most shocked by Titus's offer. Max looked dumbfounded, but only slightly more so than Titus himself. After a second, he frowned and pointed at the swirling tats on his arms. "Look, I know what people suspect about my background. That's my fault for not telling them the truth. If you think having me there wouldn't go over well with the parents, just say so. It won't hurt my feelings."

Something in his voice made her suspect that might not be true. She hastened to reassure him without being too heavy-handed about it. "It's not like you're a stranger to the people in town, and they know you and Cade are friends. That should ease any doubts they might have. From what Thomas told me, they run into more problems when one of the parents gets dragooned into umping and either makes a bunch of mistakes or doesn't seem to be impartial."

Max chimed in with, "So what you're saying is that you need someone neutral so both sides can be mad at him without feeling guilty."

He meant it as a joke, but it was probably true. "Yeah, I'd say so."

Max rubbed his hands together. "I can tag along in case Titus needs backup. I was a pretty good shortstop back in the day. I'll bring Rikki and Carter, too. I think the kid would get a kick out of watching the games. We're hoping to sign him up for T-ball in the spring."

Problem solved. "I'll call Thomas back and ask him to drop off a copy of the rule book for each of you. We should arrive at the park around four thirty. The first game is scheduled to start at five."

Titus looked surprised. "We? Are you coming, too?"

Would he rather she didn't? "I figure somebody ought to be there cheering for the umpire and his assistant."

Titus looked slightly less freaked out by what he'd just volunteered to do. "And to protect us from irate parents?"

She laughed and patted him on the arm. "That, too."

THE BASEBALL DIAMOND was located on the back side of the same park where she'd found Jimmy the previous night. Right now, the people starting to pour into the park were there to watch their kids play baseball. It had been years since Moira had attended one of her cousin's games, but she remembered having a great time hooting and hollering when one of the kids got a hit or made a great catch. She was looking forward to doing that again, but she was also concerned about Titus's role in the games. He would do his best to be both impartial and accurate with his calls. The only question was if the parents would give him a fair chance.

Since she wasn't on duty, she hoped to get lost in the crowd rather than look as if she was there in her professional capacity. With that in mind, she'd stopped off at home long enough to take a quick shower and change into civilian clothes. That was also why she'd borrowed her mother's car instead of driving her official vehicle. Unfortunately, her hope of blending in died when someone called her name as soon as she stepped out of the vehicle.

It took her a second to spot her friend Carli waving at her from across the parking lot. Moira waved back and cut through the line of cars to reach her. "I didn't expect to see you here."

Carli fell into step with her as they started down the path that led through the trees to the baseball field. "Some of the kids in the Sunday-school class that I'm teaching this year are playing today. I promised them I would come. How about you? Do you know someone in the game?"

Great. This could get awkward. She'd already been debating whether she could safely reveal to Carli that Ryan Donovan and Titus Kondrat were one and the same man. She trusted her friend's discretion, but Titus hadn't chosen to share his past with the locals for good reason.

Carli was still waiting for an answer, so Moira went with an almost accurate version of the facts. "I was in the café this morning talking to a friend. Titus Kondrat overheard me saying that I'd been asked to find someone who would be willing to umpire the games this afternoon. To my surprise, he volunteered. Since I got him into this situation, I thought I should be here to show my support."

It was too much to hope that Carli would take the explanation at face value without peppering Moira with a bunch of questions she didn't want to answer. Instead, she tugged Moira off the path, where they could talk without blocking the people coming up behind them. As soon as they were out of the way, Carli said, "Run that by me again."

"Titus is working behind the plate, and Max Volkov will be umpiring out in the field."

"So Titus was eavesdropping while you were talking to Max Volkov?"

That sounded bad for some reason. Knowing she was about to lose complete control of the conversation, Moira swallowed hard and tried again, "Actually, the three of us were sitting at the same table eating cinnamon rolls when the subject came up."

Carli did a little victory dance, a huge grin on her face. "I knew I was right. There is something going on between you and the mystery man. I want all the details."

Feeling a little panicky, Moira glanced around to see if anyone might be listening to their conversation. Most people walked by with barely a glance in their direction, but this still wasn't the time or place for this conversation. "Look, it's complicated, and I can't explain everything here. I promise I'll share what I can the next time we get together."

"Well, that's disappointing." Carli put her hands on her hips in an attempt to look intimidating. "My social calendar is wide open, so pick a night. I'm guessing you would rather not share all the details in front your mom and grandmother, so we'll meet at my place. You can even stay over if it's the kind of conversation that will require multiple bottles of wine."

"It just might."

Her voice cracked just a bit, which had

Carli frowning big-time. "Do I need to borrow some kid's bat to make sure Titus knows to toe the line when it comes to how he treats you? I won't stand for another jerk hurting you like that guy did back in the day."

It was hard not to laugh at the irony. "We'd better get moving. I don't want to miss anything."

When Carli made no move to start down the path, Moira tried again, "I told Titus and Max that we needed to be there by four thirty. I don't want them to think I bailed on them."

"We're not going anywhere until you answer my question. Do I need that bat or not? Will he treat you right?"

While Moira appreciated her friend's determination to protect her, it still wasn't a conversation she wanted to have. She and Titus weren't in a relationship, not the kind Carli was talking about. The truth was Moira didn't know what they had. Yes, they'd exchanged a couple of kisses, but those had been done on impulse. He hadn't said a word about officially getting involved again, and she wasn't sure that's what she wanted, anyway. What if they tried and it all went wrong again? Wouldn't it be better to settle for being friends? Safer, at least. That might actually be the best scenario considering they lived in such a small town.

But it would also be pretty disappointing.

CHAPTER FIFTEEN

TITUS LOOKED AROUND the baseball field and fought the urge to take off running. What had he gotten himself into? He'd spent most of the afternoon reading and rereading the rule book Thomas Kline had given him. Considering the kids in the first game were seven and eight years old, it was doubtful he'd need to know much about the more obscure rules and regulations. That didn't mean he wasn't nervous.

At least Max had called to say that he and Rikki were definitely bringing Carter to watch Max and Titus umpire the game. That was good. For sure, Thomas Kline had been relieved to learn that Moira had been able to round up two volunteers to help out. Titus figured that "two suckers" was a better description, but he'd faced tougher situations and survived. Now, if only the person who'd gotten him into this mess would show up. He could use some moral support.

He'd been on the receiving end of curious looks from some of the parents as they arrived, but no one had actually approached him. A few of the kids had stopped and stared at him in confusion, as if wondering why he was out of his normal environment at the café. It was kind of like back when he was six and ran into his first-grade teacher at the grocery story. Who knew that teachers didn't actually live at school?

"You're looking a bit freaked-out there."

He slowly turned around, trying to look far calmer than he actually felt. "It's about time you got here."

Moira jerked her head toward the bleachers. "I ran into Carli out in the parking lot. She had questions. You know, about how you happened to overhear me mentioning I needed to find an umpire for the game."

"You make it sound like I was sneaking around to listen on your conversation. As I recall, you were sitting right next to me at the time."

"Yes, I know. That information was clarified upon cross-examination. Carli has an uncanny knack for sensing when I'm not being totally honest with her."

A glance in the same direction verified her friend was watching the two of them with great interest. "And was she satisfied with your answers?"

"Not exactly. Ever since that day she and I ate lunch together at the café, she has suspected that there's something going on between the two of us. I tried denying it then, but wasn't all that successful. Probably because I don't like lying to my friends. Having said that, you haven't chosen to share your past with many people here in Dunbar. I figure that's your right, so I've danced around the subject."

She sidled up closer and whispered, "But you better be careful around Carli. She's already asked if she needed to borrow a bat. Something about using it to convince you to treat me better than that jerk Ryan Donovan did back in the day."

Great. "So she knows about him...me...us and what happened."

"She doesn't know that you're him, if that's what you're asking." Moira stared up at him, her blue eyes so solemn. "But she's the one who helped me pick up the pieces."

There was something he should be saying that would soothe the pain in that single sentence. For the life of him, he couldn't think what it might be, especially standing at the edge of a baseball diamond in front a small crowd. He kept it simple. "I promise she won't need the bat."

"Mr. Kondrat, here's your gear. I have some for the other guy, too."

Neither of them had noticed Mr. Kline's approach. At least he seemed too distracted to have been listening to their conversation. "You can leave Max's stuff with me. I'll see that he gets it."

"I've told the coaches from both games how you stepped up to help out tonight. They're pretty levelheaded as far as coaches go, so you shouldn't have any problems. If you do, I'll want to hear about it. We have rules about such things and do our best to enforce them. Sometimes people get caught up in the moment and forget baseball is a game and supposed to be fun, especially at the age these kids are."

Then he gave Titus a considering look.

"Somehow I don't think you'll run into any problems you can't handle."

Thomas winked as he looked past him to Moira. "And you have some serious backup, too."

"I'm a civilian tonight, Mr. Kline. I'm here to support Titus and Max since I got them into this, but I plan to cheer for both teams."

"Smart woman." He pointed off to the left. "Looks like your friend has arrived. I'll be around long enough to make sure the first game starts off okay. After that, I'm umpiring a game at the middle school. If you wouldn't mind taking the gear with you, I'll pick it up at your café tomorrow."

Titus nodded. "No problem, and lunch will be on me."

"That's mighty nice of you, Mr. Kondrat. I'll see you then."

By that point, Max had gotten Rikki and Carter settled in the bleachers. It looked like they'd hit the refreshment stand on the way in. Both were chowing down on hot dogs and there was a small bucket of popcorn sitting between them. Nothing like junk food to make a sporting event more fun.

After getting his wife and new son set-

ALEXIS MORGAN

tled, Max crossed the field to join him and Moira. Titus gave him his share of the gear designed to protect the umpires from fast-moving baseballs. As he began strapping on a shin guard, Max looked around before whispering, "I hope I don't make a complete fool of myself doing this."

Moira handed him the other shin guard. "Relax, Max. This isn't the big leagues, and you're both a lot bigger than the players are even if they are armed with bats. Besides, I'm betting you can outrun the little rascals."

"Thanks for making me feel better...not. We all know the parents and grandparents are the scary ones."

"True enough. And on that positive note, I should head over to the stands before Carli thinks I've forgotten about her. Good luck to both of you. Afterward, I'll buy the first round at Barnaby's. Maybe even the second."

Max finished fastening the straps on his chest protector. "Thanks for the offer, but I'll have to take a rain check. It'll be Carter's bedtime by the time we get done here. I don't like to miss story time."

It was disappointing, even if understandable, why Max would prefer to spend time with his new family. Titus hoped it didn't mean that Moira would retract the offer. He'd love a chance to spend some time with her when she wasn't on duty and they weren't surrounded by his employees and customers.

But he'd rather know now than spend the next couple of hours wondering. "Will Carli be coming, too?"

To his relief, Moira hesitated only a second before nodding. "I'll invite her, but I don't know if she has other plans."

As she walked away, Titus wondered if it was bad on his part to be hoping Carli had somewhere else she needed to be. Regardless, he was relieved that Moira seemed okay with the idea of hanging out with him at the tavern for a drink or maybe even two. Things were looking up.

IT HAD BEEN obvious that both Max and Titus were jittery before the first game started. After all, neither of them had any umpiring experience. That didn't account for why she was on the edge of her seat and as tense as any parent in the stands. It wasn't as if Moira had a child in the game to worry about. No, instead she had the umpire, a man who was perfectly able to take care of himself. If Titus could handle going undercover in a drug cartel, he could handle this situation.

She'd heard a few murmurs from people sitting around her who obviously didn't know who he was. No matter how protective she was feeling, it wasn't her job to leap to his defense. Luckily, someone else spoke up. In the process, she learned a few things about Titus that she hadn't known about, starting with how he routinely donated money to local programs for kids. As near as she could tell, the man was a soft touch whenever there was a fundraiser going on in town.

It was a sure bet he would've never told her about his efforts to support the community like that. The man liked keeping his cards close to his chest. She also couldn't help but notice that an awful lot of the players themselves knew him. It probably wasn't normal practice for the umpire to offer high fives as the kids came charging across home plate, but they seemed to expect Titus to celebrate with them. Since he did the same thing for both teams, no one could claim he played favorites. Funny how he seemed more at ease with children than he did with most adults.

Considering kids usually were pretty good judges of character, she liked what that said about him.

Max was also doing a good job dealing with the kids. She wondered if either man realized that they'd probably be getting calls the next time a substitute umpire was needed. Somehow, she doubted either of them would mind.

"You're looking pretty starry-eyed there, lady."

Moira shot a quelling look in her friend's direction. "I am not."

When Carli rolled her eyes in disbelief, Moira tried again, "I'm the one who got Max and Titus involved in this. I'm simply happy that things have gone smoothly so far. That's all."

"You keep telling yourself that. I get why you might want to convince me that's all it is, but you're not usually in the habit of lying to yourself. Seriously, I haven't seen you this interested in a man in a long time. Maybe you should ask Titus out and see how it goes."

Right then one of the players hit a home run, and the crowd went wild. Moira was excited for the kid, but she was also grateful that all the resulting hooting and hollering as he ran the bases made any further conversation impossible until the noise died down. After everyone returned to their seats, she drew a slow breath and braced herself for Carli's reaction to what she had to say next. "I already invited Titus and Max to Barnaby's for a drink after the game."

"And did they say yes? Because I'd be surprised if Max would go unless Rikki could get a babysitter at the last minute."

"He took a rain check, so it would be you, me and Titus."

Carli looked horrified by that prospect. "Oh, no. You're not roping me into chaperoning the two of you."

"It's just a drink, Carli. My way of thanking him for stepping up to help out. It's not like it's a date."

"But it could be if you'd just admit you're interested in the man." Carli kept her eyes trained on the game. When she finally spoke again, there was a heavy dose of sympathy in her voice. "Believe me, I get it, Moira. We both know it's hard to put yourself out there again, but not every guy is like Ryan or my ex."

Carli finally turned to face Moira. "I have to believe that if I ever want to be happy again. It's not that I want to dive right into something serious. It would be safer to dip my toes in the dating pool a few times to test the waters. But eventually I want someone to call my own. Someone I can trust to build a future with me, maybe even start a family."

Moira not only heard the longing in Carli's voice, but she also understood it. She told her the same thing she'd told her before. Maybe eventually Carli would believe her. "You deserve a nice guy who is smart enough to recognize how special you are."

"Ditto to you, too."

Crossing her fingers, Moira asked, "So will you come to Barnaby's with me?"

"I've never been there, but I'm pretty sure it's not my kind of place. Have you ever been there?"

Moira was fairly certain her answer wouldn't reassure her friend at all. She leaned in closer to keep this part of their conversation private. "Only professionally, and then only outside in the parking lot."

Obviously, that possibility hadn't occurred to Carli. Wide-eyed, she whispered back, "So if you've raided the place, how will the owner feel about you showing up? Won't he be unhappy about having a member of the local police hanging out there?"

"I'll be there as a private citizen. Besides, the owner has been known to call us himself when he has problems with a customer. From what Cade has said, Shay Barnaby wants his customers to enjoy themselves, but he doesn't put up with bad behavior. We usually get called to deal with the ones he's already tossed out."

"I wonder what constitutes bad behavior in a tavern that caters to a pretty rough crowd."

"Actually, I'm not sure, but I guess we'll find out. So you'll come, right?"

Carli sighed dramatically. "Fine, I'll come."

The bleachers began emptying out, signaling the second game had ended. Moira stood and stretched a few stiff muscles. She'd forgotten how uncomfortable it was to sit on wooden bleacher seats for so long. Once the exodus slowed down, she and Carli made their way to the field, where Titus and Max were stripping off their gear and stuffing it back into the duffels Mr. Kline had provided. Rikki and her son stood nearby, the little boy talking a mile a minute to Titus. From the sound of it, this had been the first real ball game he'd ever seen.

"And I had two hot dogs and popcorn and a purple snow cone!"

Titus took suitably impressed as he kneeled down to better hear Carter in the midst of the crowd. "Sounds like you liked the food even more than the game."

The little guy frowned as he gave the matter some thought. "I liked watching Dad a lot. You, too, Mr. Titus. Mom and me think you both did a good job."

Titus ruffled Carter's hair. "I'm glad you think so. It was our first time umpiring, so it was a bit scary."

For some reason, the little boy thought that was hilarious. "You shouldn't have been scared of a bunch of kids."

Titus's gravelly voice was laced with amusement. "It wasn't the kids I was scared of. It was the parents. Sometimes they don't think the umpires are being fair to their kids and yell at them."

"Then they're being mean. You'd never be unfair."

Then the little guy held out his arms to

offer Titus a hug. She wasn't sure how he would respond, but he swept Carter up and hugged him back. Whatever he whispered to him restored the boy's happy smile. When he set him back down on the ground, Max and Rikki each took one of Carter's hands. Rikki smiled at Titus. "You'll have to come for dinner soon, Titus. Carter and Max built another model together. This one is a wooden clipper ship."

"Let me know when."

"We will." Max looked down at Carter. "Come on, kiddo. It's almost story time, and I've been waiting all day to find out what happens in the next chapter."

After the trio headed off for the parking lot, Moira waited until Titus picked up the two duffels and slung the straps over his shoulder before speaking. "Are you still up for having a drink with the two of us?"

He nodded. "Sounds good to me. Can I hitch a ride with you? I walked over from the café."

"Sure thing." She turned to Carli. "Do you want to ride with us or would you prefer to drive yourself?"

"I'd better take my car. I don't want to leave it here in the parking lot after the park closes."

"Good thinking."

Even if that meant Moira would have to be alone with Titus for the time it took to get to Barnaby's. "If we get there first, we'll wait for you outside."

"Okay. Also, I have church in the morning, so I won't be able to stay long."

"You're not the only one. I'm back on the day shift."

Titus entered the conversation. "Look, I know you think you owe me for helping out with the game. If you'd rather not do this, just say so. I know all about how hard it is to work all day after a late night."

Gosh, how could she have forgotten that he'd been up late helping her out last night and still had to be ready bright and early to open the café on time? "I'm sorry, Titus. I forgot that you've got to be running on fumes by now. We can reschedule. Your choice."

He stared at her for what felt like a long time before he finally answered, "Actually, I could use a cold one. And what do you say we add in some of Shay's hot wings? I've been trying to get him to share his recipe, but the selfish jerk won't even give me a hint."

Feeling like she was about to do a high dive without knowing how deep the water was, Moira found herself grinning. "I say yes."

CHAPTER SIXTEEN

TITUS SETTLED INTO the front seat of the car and tried to get comfortable. There wasn't quite enough legroom for a man of his height, but they didn't have all that far to go. A few minutes into the ride, he noticed Moira's white-knuckled grip on the steering wheel. He had no doubt she likely had second thoughts about this outing. She also kept checking the rear-view mirror to make sure her friend hadn't changed her mind about joining them. If that happened, he figured there was better than a fifty-fifty chance that Moira would suddenly think of something at work that required her immediate attention.

That would be disappointing but not surprising. He'd known he was playing with fire by accepting Moira's impulsive invitation to join her and Carli for a drink and some hot wings at Barnaby's. Considering how antsy both of the ladies were acting, he had to wonder if either of them had ever been in Barnaby's before tonight. That would certainly explain Carli's nervousness about the situation. Maybe Moira's, too, but he suspected that had more to do with the push-pull nature of her relationship with him.

Moira could handle anything that happened at the bar, but he had concerns about Carli. Still, Shay never let things get too far out of hand. Early on, he'd posted a short list of rules that he expected to be followed or else. It hadn't taken long for Shay's customers to learn that the former Recon Marine was a man of his word.

"We're here."

Titus sat up taller and looked around. He'd been so lost in his thoughts that he hadn't realized they'd arrived. "Is Carli still with us?"

"Yeah, she parked two spots down from where we are." Moira looked a little uneasy. "I'm guessing she won't stay long, but don't take it personally. She went through an ugly divorce a while back. Her ex already had his next wife waiting in the wings before he even told Carli he wanted out of their marriage. From what I heard, he married the woman the day after the divorce was finalized, and his new wife gave birth to their first child three weeks later. All of that has left Carli a bit skittish when it comes to dating or meeting new men."

That explained a few things. "I kind of got that impression. It's taken some time, but she's finally quit jumping whenever I approach her in the café. I was hoping I wasn't actually that scary. That would be bad for business."

Moira smiled at that last part as he hoped she would. He barely knew Carli, but even the brief description of what she'd gone through had him wanting to punch something. He flexed his hands several times to work off some of the tension. "She has to know she's so much better off without that guy. That doesn't mean I wouldn't like to give him a hands-on lecture on how a man should treat his woman."

Not that he had much room to talk considering how he deceived Moira ten years ago.

She started to open her door but stopped to look back at him. "I'm sworn to uphold the law, so I probably shouldn't admit to what I'm about to say. When I found out what happened, I asked friends of mine to keep an eye on Carli's ex. You'd be surprised by how many times he got nailed for speeding the first couple of months after he left her."

When they both got out of the car, he stopped to grin at her over the roof of the car. "Good for you. Does she know?"

"Nope. I'm not even sure she would have approved. She's not normally a vindictive person."

He snorted at her assessment of her friend. "Sorry, but isn't she the one who offered to borrow a bat in case I needed a reminder to treat you right?"

She offered him a wide-eyed, innocent look. "Yep, come to think of it, she did. Well, what can I say? Women are complicated."

At that point, Carli joined them. She looked at Moira and then at Titus. "What's so funny?"

Titus immediately clamped his mouth shut and left it up to Moira to explain. "Um, we were just laughing about something someone said at the ball game."

Moira was complicated all right; she was also sneaky. Technically, she wasn't even lying to her friend since Carli had made the comment about borrowing the bat at the park.

Meanwhile, Moira looped her arm through Carli's. "Come on, let's head inside. I've been craving those hot wings ever since Titus mentioned them."

Carli glanced at Titus, looking a bit concerned. "Are they really that hot? I don't like things that are too spicy."

Titus hastened to reassure her. "That's not a problem. Shay offers them with different levels of heat, which are rated from one through five. We can order the mildest version."

Moira wasn't having it. "Nope, not for me. I like them hot."

They'd reached the door. As he hustled ahead to open it for them, Titus tried one more time to warn Moira that she might be biting off more than she could chew...literally. "You probably won't believe me, but I've seen grown men cry after biting into the hottest ones. You might want to start with the threes and work your way up from there."

The stubborn woman scoffed as she headed inside. "You two can play it safe if you want to, but I'm more of a go-big-or-go-home kind of girl."

"Don't say I didn't warn you."

He followed her toward an empty table near

the front of the bar. The music was blasting loud enough to make conversation difficult while they were on the move. When they were seated, he studied the list of all of the available microbrews. Good, it looked like Shay had added a couple of new ones to the menu since the last time Titus had stopped in.

Moira plucked the list from his hand and studied it before passing it over to her friend. He wasn't surprised when Carli checked out the pitifully short list of wines that Shay bothered to keep on hand. The bar's usual clientele tended to go for beer or the hard stuff. People who preferred wine normally headed to somewhere fancier in one of the bigger towns in the area. After a bit, Carli wrinkled her nose and set the list back down on the table.

It was a bit of a surprise when Shay himself appeared to take their order. "It's been a while, Titus."

"I've been busy."

The truth was the bar was often too loud and too crowded for his personal tastes. Meanwhile, he performed the necessary introductions. Shay smiled at Carli first. "Welcome to Barnaby's, Ms. Walsh."

When she nodded, he turned his attention

to Moira. "And, Officer Fraser, it's nice to finally meet you in person."

She smiled at him. "Please call me Moira."

Since Titus usually came in alone, he was surprised when Shay didn't ask how he'd been lucky enough to show up with two attractive women this time. It would've been funny to see his reaction to finding out that Moira wanted to buy Titus a drink for umpiring a kids' ball game. Instead, Shay was still playing the role of good host to new guests to his establishment. "So what can I get y'all?"

Titus didn't know where Shay was from originally, but he suspected it was someplace well south of the Mason-Dixon Line. He'd heard more than one woman exclaim over his soft drawl and good manners. It hadn't even occurred to Titus that he would be introducing Moira to one of the few eligible men in Dunbar. It might not be the smartest thing he'd ever done considering the unpredictable nature of his relationship with her. It was definitely time to place their order, so Shay could move on to his other customers. "I'll have that new pale ale on the menu. Moira, what would you like?"

"I'll have the same."

Shay jumped in to ask Carli himself, no doubt noting she was back to studying his limited wine list. "And what can I get for you, Ms. Walsh? I stock a decent red, but I also have a new Riesling I'm trying out that's not on the list yet. It's not too dry, but not too sweet, either."

Carli set aside the menu and offered Shay a shy smile. "I'll have a glass of that. Thank you."

He smiled back. "Let me know what you think."

"I will."

Titus noticed one of the bartenders was desperately trying to get Shay's attention and pointed back toward the bar. "Looks like you're being paged, Shay."

He shot his employee an exasperated look and bellowed, "Hold your horses, Jody! I'll be there in a minute." Then, bringing his attention back to Moira and Carli, he turned down the volume on his voice. "Sorry about that. Can I get anything else for you folks?"

Titus figured he'd give Moira one last chance to show some common sense. "Carli and I will split an order of the mildest hot wings."

Then he pointed toward Moira. "This one insists she wants the hottest ones."

Shay blinked in surprise. "Are you sure? Usually the only people who order those are the ones who've lost a bet of some kind."

At least his explanation gave her pause for thought. "They're that hot?"

"Yes, ma'am, they are." Shay grinned at her. "I'll tell you what—if you'll go with an order of the threes, I'll throw in one of the fives for comparison."

This time Moira didn't hesitate. "It's a deal."

Titus waited until Shay walked away, then muttered, "Smart move, but how come you believed him and not me?"

He'd love to know the answer to that question, but Carli derailed that conversation by pointing to a neon sign on the wall. "I've never heard of a bar that has a written standard of conduct."

Then she glanced around as if checking to make sure that Shay wasn't close by. "I assume Mr. Barnaby is the one who posted it, but was he serious?"

Moira answered before Titus could. "Yeah, Cade said the number of times that we have to deal with problems here has gone way down since people realized what happens when someone doesn't follow Shay's rules."

Carli looked around the bar with great interest. "Remember back on my twenty-first birthday when you, me and some other friends were going to go out for drinks to celebrate? My folks made me promise that we'd go anywhere other than this place."

Moira grinned at her. "Growing up here, we all heard tales about the shenanigans that happened here." Then she gave Titus a considering look. "I think an argument could be made that it hasn't changed all that much."

Feeling obligated to defend himself, Titus leaned back in his chair and crossed his arms over his chest. "Shay has never had cause to toss me out of this place. Isn't that right?"

He directed that question to the man himself, who had just walked up to the table. "That's true. Titus is always on his best behavior whenever he comes in. A model citizen and inspiration to us all. In fact, if I ever get around to posting a customer honor roll, he'll be right up there near the top."

Even Titus had to laugh at that, although he was pretty sure Shay hadn't necessarily meant it as a compliment. Meanwhile, Shay unloaded the tray one of his servers was holding. "Here are your drinks, your wings and my dinner."

He carefully handed Carli her wine and then set beers in front of Titus, Moira and himself. What the heck was Shay doing? No one had issued him an invitation to join them. Moira looked a little surprised, but she didn't say anything. Neither did Carli, but then maybe they thought this was normal behavior for Shay.

Once he was settled in, Shay met Titus's gaze, a glint of amusement in his expression. "Sorry if I'm intruding, but I decided it was unfair for Titus to keep the two prettiest ladies in here all to himself."

Carli immediately blushed while Moira rolled her eyes, which made Shay laugh. "I also wanted to be close at hand if you ran into problems with that hot wing I promised you. It's not too late to change your mind."

MOIRA LOOKED FIRST at Shay and then at Titus. The bar owner looked amused, but Titus not so much. Meanwhile, the server was back, this time with a tall glass of milk. Shay took it and leaned across the table to set it next to Moira's personal basket of wings. "The one in the separate wrapper is the hot one. Normally we ring the bell to announce someone is about to do something entertaining. However, I'll save you that particular embarrassment, Moira."

"Thanks a lot, Shay."

He laughed at the distinct lack of sincerity in her words. "You're welcome. I will, however, wish you good luck."

There was no dignified way to get out of the corner she'd backed herself into. Bracing herself as she prepared to release an inferno in her mouth, she picked up the wing and took a respectable bite out of it. Then she waited for the burn to begin. Seconds passed with only a mild tingle teasing her tongue and lips.

It wasn't until she finally looked up at Shay that she knew she'd been had. "Cute, Mr. Barnaby. How many people fall for that trick on any given night?"

He cracked up, his deep laughter ringing out across the room, drawing far more attention to their table than she was comfortable with. "Actually, none. Normally, I give people what they ask for. But you looked like you might be having second thoughts and I opted to let you rethink your decision. That one was a two, but the rest are level threes. If those aren't hot enough, next time we'll know to serve you the fours."

Then he jerked his head in Titus's direction. "Besides, your guy was looking a little bit worried."

She started to protest that Titus wasn't her anything, but she doubted it would convince Shay that his assessment of the situation was wrong. Heck, she couldn't even convince herself of that. At least he'd turned his attention to the man in question.

Shay flexed his shoulders, giving his already impressive muscles a little more definition. "While I don't mind a good dustup now and then, even I would have second thoughts about taking Titus on."

He was joking. She hoped so, anyway. While Moira was used to dealing with some pretty tough characters, it dawned on her to wonder how this particular exchange was affecting the fourth member of their party. She got her answer when Carli abruptly stood. "Hey, are you okay?"

Her friend's smile looked a little brittle.

"Yes, but it's time I headed home. Like I said before, I have to be up early in the morning."

Carli turned her attention to Shay. "You were right about the wine. I liked it quite a lot. It was nice meeting you."

Wow, her friend sounded as if she meant that. Moira wanted to ask if that was true, but now wasn't the time or place. "I'll walk you out to your car."

Her friend waved her off. "No, you don't have to do that. Stay and enjoy yourself. I'll be fine."

Before she'd gone two steps, Shay was up and moving. "I'll see you out. I prefer that our lady customers never have to walk out by themselves."

Carli pointed toward the list of Shay's rules. "I don't see that rule listed on the board."

He gave her a flirtatious grin. "It will be when I eventually get version two-point-oh posted."

The couple continued toward the door still bickering about the subject until they disappeared from sight. Moira didn't know what to make of the interaction. "What just happened?"

Titus shrugged. "I'm not sure, but you can

trust Shay. He'll see that she reaches her car safely."

Moira was inclined to believe that. She suspected Shay had a big dose of the same protective nature as Titus did. It was one of the many reasons she was finding it nearly impossible to maintain a friends-only relationship with him. She gave in to the temptation to scoot her chair closer to his and play with fire by giving his bicep a quick squeeze. He looked a little surprised by her bold move, but then he grinned and flexed the muscles in his arm.

She let her hand slide down to his forearm and asked him one more question. "So was Shay right? Should he be worried if the two of you ever came to blows?"

Titus stared at her hand as she slowly traced one of his tattoos with a fingertip. "It's best we never find out."

She withdrew her hand and feigned a stern look. "Speaking as a member of local law enforcement, I heartily agree. Now, let's finish our wings. Tomorrow is a workday for both of us."

CHAPTER SEVENTEEN

TITUS OPENED ONE of the packets that came with the hot wings and used the wipe to clean the sticky sauce off his fingers. Moira finished the last of her wings and did the same. "I can see why you'd like to steal Shay's recipe. Those are some of the best wings I've ever had."

She pushed the basket toward the center of the table and looked past him at the door. "Shay's back already, so it must have been quiet out in the parking lot tonight."

Titus shrugged. "No one would dare mess with Carli with Shay offering her his personal protection."

Once again, Shay didn't wait for an invitation and parked himself across from Moira. "I watched until your friend drove out of sight to make sure she got away safely."

Moira offered him a bright smile. "Thanks for doing that. I'm sure she appreciated it."

That actually had Shay laughing. "You would've thought so. Instead, she spent most of the time telling me she was a grown woman and perfectly capable of finding her car in a parking lot all on her own. When I tried to open her car door for her, she actually told me to back off."

Titus couldn't help but smirk a little. "She must be immune to all that Southern charm of yours I've heard so much about."

"At least some folks think I have some charm." Shay gave him a superior look. "That's more than I can say about you. Frankly, I'm amazed your café does as well as it does considering your reputation for growling at people."

Sadly, that was a fairly accurate assessment of Titus's personality, but as far as he could tell, Moira didn't mind his less-than-sunny disposition. Meanwhile, Shay caught the attention of one of the servers and then stacked up the basket that held his half-eaten dinner and the two that had held the hot wings. When she reached the table, he handed them to her and then pointed at the empty bottles. "The next round is on me."

Moira shook her head. "Sorry, but I probably shouldn't have another drink since I'm driving."

Shay didn't argue and instead switched gears. "Bring coffee instead along with a fresh burger and fries for me. Get them another basket of mild wings, too."

Titus was never good at small talk, but Shay seemed all too willing to take on that role. "So, Moira, how do you like policing a small town after working in the big city? I bet things seem a bit dull after everything you must have dealt with in Seattle."

She scrunched her nose a little. "I wouldn't call it dull, just different. I also like being close to my family. They're a big part of the reason I moved back to Dunbar."

"I get that. When I decided to leave the military behind, I wasn't sure what I wanted to do next. Inheriting this place made the decision for me. That I have an aunt and a few other relatives scattered around the area was a bonus."

Shay turned his attention to Titus. "I don't think I've ever heard how you ended up in Dunbar."

Moira bit her lower lip, maybe trying to hold back a laugh. She knew full well why he had moved to Dunbar, but also that story wasn't something Titus was in the habit of sharing with just anyone. He settled for a partial version of the truth. "I wasn't happy working in fancy restaurants and wanted to find a small café where I could get to know my customers. I also liked the Pacific Northwest and living near the mountains, so Dunbar fit the bill. I guess I'm a small-town guy at heart."

Shay looked a bit doubtful, but he didn't say anything. Luckily, their food arrived, putting a hold on the need for any further conversation. Titus wasn't hungry for more wings, so he concentrated on drinking his coffee. Moira made more of an effort to enjoy the wings while Shay devoured his dinner. No doubt he was used to having to make quick work of a meal while he had the chance.

When he finished off the last of his fries, he studied the small dance floor, where several couples were giving it their all to some fast-paced country song. Then he gave Moira a considering look. "Any chance you'd like to dance?"

Titus wished he'd thought of asking her first, but he didn't say anything. He didn't own Moira and knew she wouldn't take it well if he let his inner caveman loose in the bar. He sipped his coffee as Moira glanced toward the other couples and then back to their host. "Why not?"

Shay escorted her to the dance floor just as another song started. Titus's fingers ached from the tight grip he had on his cup. At least it wasn't a slow dance. He watched Moira and Shay as they quickly found their rhythm together. A smile lit up her face, making her even more beautiful, even if it wasn't directed at him. That thought had him up and moving toward the jukebox. After scanning the choices, he stuffed several quarters in the slot and impatiently waited for the current song to end.

Before the last note died away, he was across the dance floor holding his hand out to Moira. He let out a slow breath when she didn't hesitate to take it. When Shay didn't immediately retreat, Titus tugged Moira in close to his side, but didn't say a single word. Instead of taking offense, Shay laughed. "I'm surprised you waited this long."

"Don't be a jerk."

"Sorry, but I have to go with my strengths."

Then Shay aimed a large dose of his Southern charm in Moira's direction. "Thank you for the dance and the info. Enjoy your dance with this guy."

As Titus swung her into his arms, she gave him a puzzled look. "Do you two not get along?"

"We do most of the time." He stared past her to where Shay was leaning against the bar and watching their every move. When he realized Titus had noticed, he laughed and turned his back to focus his attention on whatever the bartender was telling him. "Tonight he's just having fun poking the bear. I think he's jealous that I'm here with the prettiest woman in the place."

He twirled her out and back in again. "So what info was he talking about?"

Moira looked around, probably wanting to make sure Shay wasn't close enough to hear their discussion. "He asked a few questions about Carli."

So Shay was interested Carli. That was a relief, even if Moira didn't seem all that happy about it. "What did you tell him?"

"The truth about her situation."

"Which is?"

"That Carli is still getting over a bad breakup and taking things slow. You know, basically being pretty selective about the kinds of guys she wants to date."

He bet that went over well with Shay. The man also wasn't the kind to give up easily if he was interested in Carli. For some odd reason, Titus felt obligated to defend him. "You know Shay's not a bad guy, and he's very protective of the women who work here."

"I told him that I'd heard that about him. I just didn't want him to take it personally if she's not interested in going out with him."

Of course, Shay would take it personally. Who wouldn't? Not that Titus was going to argue with her. For the moment, he didn't care about Shay or even Carli. He wanted to enjoy this dance with this woman. His woman, whether she knew it or not.

Apparently, Moira wasn't done with the discussion. "Carli is an adult and can make her own choices, but I still worry about her. Her ex did a real number on her self-esteem, and I think she needs someone who will take things slow and treat her well. The proverbial nice guy next door."

Considering how Carli had argued with

Shay all the way out to her car, Titus had to wonder if Moira's assessment was on target, but it wasn't like he claimed to be an expert when it came to women. The one thing he knew for a fact, though, was that having Moira back in his arms felt perfect.

The song finally came to an end. When Moira started to step back, he held on to her hand. "One more dance, and then we should probably head out."

When the music started up again, a slow ballad this time, she studied him for a few seconds before closing the distance between them to rest her head against his shoulder. They fell into an easy rhythm as if they'd danced together forever. It had been the same way the night they first met, and he'd missed it every day since. Her soft sigh made him hope that she had, too.

They swayed slowly as the singer told a story of heartbreak and dreaming of second chances. Maybe it had been a bit heavy-handed on his part to pick that song, but he hadn't been able to resist. "This is nice."

She didn't say anything for the longest time, but neither did she try to put any distance between them. Finally, as the last notes of the song faded away, she murmured, "Yeah, it is."

Maybe it was time to push for something more. "We should do this again sometime soon. Maybe head into Seattle and make an evening of it."

Before she could respond, Shay was back and holding out her phone. "You left this on the table. Someone is trying to reach you."

She checked the call log. "It's Oscar. I've got to call him back."

Shay pointed toward the hallway that led toward the restrooms. "If you need someplace more private, you can use my office. It's across from the ladies room."

"Thanks, Shay."

Moira was off and running. So much for spending any more time together. He and Shay wandered back to the table to wait for Moira to return. There was always a chance that Oscar only needed to ask her a question or something.

"So you and her…"

Shay didn't finish the sentence, but he didn't have to. Titus kept his answer simple. "Working on it."

"I can see why. I like her."

"So do I."

Shay leaned back in his seat, arms crossed over his chest. "A cop seems like an odd choice for you, what with your reputation and all."

"You mean the one where people think I got my ink in prison and also learned how to cook there?"

The other man laughed. "Yeah, that one."

"Next time you stop in the café, remind me to show you my diploma from the culinary school where I got my degree."

"I might just do that. But for the record, I never believed the prison theory. It never rang true to me."

Interesting. Most people bought in to the rumors without hesitation. "Why not?"

"I haven't known Cade Peters for long, but the man is definitely a straight arrow. I can't see him being best buddies with an ex-con."

Titus huffed a small laugh. "It could just be that he loves my chicken and dumplings too much to risk offending me."

"Couldn't blame him for that. I also don't think Moira would've enjoyed a slow dance with a man who has a shady character." Shay focused on something back over Titus's shoulder and then met his gaze head-on again. "I'm not asking for details about your past. We all have secrets. I'm just saying that of all the people in Dunbar, you've ended up with two cops as friends. Makes me wonder what you might have in common with them."

Then he stood up. "But that's a conversation for another day. Your lady is headed back this way."

When Titus reached for his wallet, Shay waved him off. "Forget it. You can treat me to some of those chicken and dumplings I've heard so much about."

Titus tossed some cash on the table to tip their server. "That's the Thursday special, so make sure you come in early enough to get some or call and let me know to put some back for you."

"Will do. Thanks for coming in tonight. Bring the ladies back anytime."

He walked away before Moira reached the table. "We should go. Oscar is tied up on a call that will take another hour or so to handle. I need to cover until the next shift starts. I'll drop you off at home."

"No need. I can walk if you can drop the

duffels off at the café in the morning for Mr. Kline to pick up."

Still, she hesitated. "If you're sure. It's pretty late to be out and about."

"My house is only a fifteen-minute walk from here. I'll be fine."

Outside, he followed Moira over to where she'd left her car. "Are you going to snap at me like Carli did at Shay when he wanted to open her door for her?"

"I guess we'll have to see."

She pushed the button on her key to unlock the car. But instead of leaving immediately, she leaned back against the car and stared up at the sky. After a few seconds, she let out a slow breath. "Tonight was fun."

He inched closer to her. "It was. Well, except for watching you dancing with Shay. I could have done without that."

She gave him a curious look. "Would you have asked me to dance if he hadn't?"

Feeling he was about to step on a land mine, he gave her the honest answer. "I would have if I'd known you would actually say yes."

He expected her to laugh or maybe roll her eyes, but her expression turned serious. "I'm

pretty sure I wouldn't have been able to resist."

Well, that was encouraging. He traced the
line of her cheek with a fingertip. "And if I
asked you to kiss me now, would you?"

Her mouth quirked up in a small smile.
"Oh, I don't know. I should get back out on
patrol."

That wasn't a definite no, but he couldn't
delay her much longer. "Then we better get
down to business."

He kept the kiss gentle and on the innocent
end of the scale. Now wasn't the time to push
for more. She tasted so sweet, and it felt so
right when she wrapped her arms around his
neck. Like coming home. Like there might be
a future for them. Like maybe she was starting to forgive him for all of the mistakes he'd
made in the past.

He savored the moment for a little longer
before stepping back. "I haven't forgotten that
you never answered me when I mentioned the
two of us going out on a real date."

She pretended to think about it as she
opened her car door. "No, I guess I didn't."

"Well?"

Her answering smile was all tease. "I'll think about it. I'll see you in the morning."

Just knowing that was true made him surprisingly happy. "Stay safe out there, Officer Fraser."

"I'll do my best."

He closed her door for her and watched as she drove off into the night. When her car disappeared from sight, he started for home. Ned wasn't going to be happy with him for staying gone so long, but Titus could buy his forgiveness with a couple of treats. As he walked, he couldn't help but wonder if he could sway Moira's decision about the whole date thing with another chocolate pie.

It was worth a shot.

CHAPTER EIGHTEEN

MOIRA WAS DEAD tired and ready for the night to be over. Oscar had finally finished the call that had kept him tied up for several hours, but then he got an emergency call on the other side of town. At this point, there wasn't much use in her going home, considering she was due back at the office in just a couple of hours.

She turned at the next corner, planning on doing another circle through town before returning to the station. But when she spotted a familiar figure walking down the sidewalk, she sped up until she drew even with him. Rolling down the passenger window, she called out, "Titus, why are you still out walking? Is everything okay?"

He walked another couple of steps before finally stopping. "I can't find Ned. He wasn't at home when I got back. He was in the house when I left for the park, but he has a doggy door so he can hang out in the backyard. Maybe he jumped the fence again. But even if he did, he never stays gone this long."

Titus ran his hands through his hair in frustration. "I thought I'd better go looking for him."

"Get in. We can cover more territory driving than you can walking."

She wasn't sure he would do as she suggested, but he finally opened the passenger door and climbed in. "I'm worried something might have happened to him."

There was no mistaking the fear in his voice. "We'll find him."

She probably shouldn't make that promise, but right now she'd do anything to ease Titus's pain. "Let me know if you see anything you want to check out. We can also use the spotlight if that will help."

"I'm probably overreacting, but he's never stayed gone this long." He pounded his fist on his thigh in frustration. "I should've gone straight home from work. If I'd done that instead of umpiring the games, he'd be home safe and sound."

Moira winced. Was she supposed to apologize or something? It wasn't as if she twisted his arm into helping out. He was the one who volunteered. Besides, he'd had a good time cheering on the kids. If he'd been that concerned about leaving Ned alone, he could have also gone straight home after the games ended. Rather than point any or all of that out, she kept her mouth shut and kept driving. It was better to cut the man some slack, especially considering both of them were operating on minimal sleep.

Right now, finding Ned was all that mattered.

They rode in silence, going slowly so she could safely check out her side of the road as he scanned the right side. As they approached the intersection ahead, she asked, "Which way now?"

He closed his eyes and drew a slow breath. "I have no idea. I've been up and down this whole area multiple times already."

The ambient light in the car cast his face in harsh shadows. Hating how worried he looked, she considered their options. "Let's drive by the café in case he's waiting for you there. He's done that before, hasn't he?"

"Yeah, he has, although most of the time

he either rides to work with me or we walk together."

"It's worth checking. After that, I'll drive you home to see if he's already found his way back. No matter what, you should try to catch some sleep."

"I'll probably shower and change clothes. I have to be back at work in a couple of hours. Once things are up and running, I'll go back out looking again."

"I'll let the officers on duty know to keep an eye out for Ned. You've probably already thought of this, but don't forget to call the shelters, too. Someone may have picked him up."

"I'll put up some notices in town if he doesn't show up soon."

A few minutes later, they circled the block around the café, but there was no sign of Ned anywhere. She had an awful feeling that their luck wouldn't be any better at Titus's house, but she kept her fingers crossed that she was wrong about that.

Titus was out of her car and charging toward his front porch before they even came to a complete stop. She turned off the engine and followed after him. He cupped his mouth and yelled, "Ned, you get yourself home right now!"

When there was no response, he tried one more time. "No treats for a week for worrying Moira like this, you worthless dog!"

They both stood in silence, hoping for some sign that the dog would respond. After a few seconds, Titus's shoulders slumped in defeat. "Like I said, thanks for trying to help, but you'd better go. You have better things to do than haul me around."

"I'll be back on duty soon. Let me know if Ned shows up."

"I will."

She started to walk away. She'd gone a few steps when Titus caught up with her. "Look, what I said earlier in the car was just me blowing off steam. I don't regret helping out at the games, and I enjoyed hanging out with you and Carli at Shay's place."

"Call if you need me."

"I will."

He started back toward the house but stopped again. "I'm not used to having anyone to care about, and I'm obviously not very good at it. I screwed up big-time ten years ago, and I'm doing it again with Ned. It might not have seemed like it at the time, but you got off lucky when things didn't work out for us."

His words hit her hard. "That's not true, Titus."

She stepped close enough to place her hand on his back. She hoped her touch would offer some comfort, but he shrugged it off. "You'd better get going. You've wasted enough time on me for one night. Maybe even for a lifetime."

His words sent a shaft of pain right through the heart of her. "Don't talk like that, Titus."

"Why not? It's the truth."

When he walked away again, she had no choice but to let him go.

TITUS MADE QUICK work of his shower and changing clothes. After that, he settled on the couch and tried to come up with a plan of action, to do something—anything—to help bring Ned home. With his nerves stretched to the breaking point, he did his best to relax in the hope that even a short nap would get his brain back to firing on all cylinders, which didn't work at all. He'd been right when he'd told Moira that he wouldn't be able to sleep.

Not when every sound, every creak of the house, had him up checking the front porch to see if it was Ned out there wanting in.

Finally, he gave up and did the only productive thing he could think of. After uploading a recent picture of Ned, he designed one of those depressing lost-pet notices to post around town. He offered a reward for any information at all. Good news would be preferable, but even the alternative would be better than not knowing. After printing off a few copies, he headed out the door to post a few on his way to the café. If Max stopped by for his usual coffee and breakfast sandwich, he'd ask him to post a few as well.

It wasn't much of a plan, but it was all he had. Darn that dog, anyway. How dare he worm his way into Titus's life only to disappear again? He couldn't wait to give the fur ball a piece of his mind as soon as he came strolling back home.

If he came home at all.

Outside, the sun was just starting to crest the horizon, but the darkness suited Titus's mood better. He'd have to warn Gunner and the rest of the staff that it would be better if he didn't have to deal with the public any more than absolutely necessary today. That would make more work for the others, but it would be easier for them in the long run.

He managed to hang about ten of his notices before he gave up and hustled the rest of the way to the café, arriving about fifteen minutes later than normal. Gunner was already hard at work in the kitchen. Keeping his back toward Titus, he grumbled, "Must be nice to sleep in on a workday. I guess that's one of the privileges of being the boss man."

When Titus didn't respond, Gunner finally turned around. He immediately wiped his hands on a towel and started toward him. "What's happened?"

"Ned is gone. I spent most of the night looking for him. There's no sign of him anywhere."

Gunner pulled out one of the chairs at the small table in the corner and all but shoved Titus down on it. "Stay put while I fix you something to eat."

"I'm not hungry."

"Tough. You haven't slept, you've got a full day of work ahead of you and then you'll be back out on the street hunting for Ned."

Instead of walking away, Gunner fidgeted

in place for a few seconds. "I might complain about Ned being underfoot all the time, but I don't mean it. He's a good dog, and when I finish my shift I'll hit the street and do some looking myself. Between all of us, we'll find him."

Before Titus could manage to string together any kind of rational reply, Gunner stalked off and started slamming pans around. In a matter of few minutes, he was back with a plate full of scrambled eggs, fresh fruit and buttered toast. On his second trip, he brought a large cup of black coffee and a glass of orange juice.

"That should hold you for a while. Let me know if you need anything else."

Titus stared at the plate for a few seconds before he finally picked up his fork and dug in. Gunner wouldn't expect him to gush over his meal, but the least he could do was make a serious effort to clean his plate.

As it turned out, Gunner was right. The food replenished Titus's energy, at least enough so that he could get started on his usual routine at the café. He started by brewing fresh coffee and making sure they had enough sets of silverware rolled up in napkins to get them through the early morning rush. As he made a few more, he heard Gunner talking to Rita and Beth. The resulting cries of dismay made it clear what he'd told the two sisters. Two seconds later, they were headed his way.

He didn't know what he expected them to say or do, but having both of them hug him at the same time was definitely a big surprise. While he got along with all of his employees, he wasn't much of a touchy-feely kind of guy. Still, it felt good to hang on to them for a few seconds. Finally, he released them and stepped back.

Rita's eyes were suspiciously shiny. "I'm so sorry, Titus. You must be worried sick about Ned. This isn't like him."

"He was a stray when he moved in with me. Maybe he decided it was time for him to find a better gig somewhere else."

Rather than agree with him, Rita shook her finger at him. "I can't believe you said that, Titus Kondrat. Everybody knows that dog loves you. We'll organize a search and find him. Just you wait and see! Your friend Max will help. Moira, too. Make some posters, and we'll plaster the town with them."

It was hard to talk around the lump in his throat. "I already started on that this morning."

"Good. Now, go open up before those folks start pounding on the door to get in."

She gave him a gentle shove to get him moving. "I know it's easy to tell someone not to worry, but you'll get through the day with our help. If Ned shows up on his own, we'll all take turns yelling at him and then stuff him full of treats. If he still hasn't come back by the time we get off work, then we'll kick the search into high gear. You're not alone in this. We all love Ned."

He jerked his head in a small nod and headed toward the door as ordered. To his surprise, Rita called after him, "And in case you don't already know it, we love you, too."

That surprise announcement had him stumbling over his own two feet. At the last second, he caught his balance. That saved him the indignity of falling flat on his face in front of not only his staff, but also the line of customers staring at him through the front windows. Maybe things were taking a turn for the better.

THANK GOODNESS THE morning all but flew by. He wasn't sure how many more words of sympathy or pats on the back he could handle without exploding. Yeah, everyone meant well, but he wasn't used to such an outpouring of support and didn't know how to deal with it. At some point, Rita had run off more copies of Ned's poster and handed them out to any customer who was willing to post a few in their neighborhood. Again, the number of people who stepped up to bat for Titus and his missing pet was a bit staggering.

He did his best to accept the sympathy in the spirit of how it was offered. That didn't mean he was comfortable with all the attention. It was a huge relief when his phone rang, and he saw it was Moira calling. He smiled—sort of, anyway—at the two elderly ladies who were fussing over him at that moment. "I'm sorry, ladies, but I have to take this call."

"We'll be praying for you and Ned, Mr. Kondrat."

"Thank you."

He held the door open for them as he answered the call. "Moira, what's up?"

"I know this probably isn't a good time, but I need you to come look at something. Can

I pick you up in two minutes? It shouldn't take long."

His heart about stopped. There was only one reason he could think of that would have her asking him to leave the café just as the lunch rush was about to start.

"Yeah, I can. But why? What's happened? Have you found him?"

"No, I haven't. Cross your fingers, but there may have been a break in the case."

"What kind of break?"

"I'm not completely sure, but keep your hopes up. I'm on my way."

CHAPTER NINETEEN

MOIRA COULD HAVE told Titus more on the phone, but she was less than two blocks away. By the time she turned down the alley behind the café, he was already outside pacing back and forth across the narrow expanse. He stopped as soon as he spotted her headed his way. Just as he had the night before, he yanked open the passenger door before she had even brought the big vehicle to a complete stop.

As she waited for him to get settled in and his seat belt fastened, someone rapped on her window, startling her. She breathed a sigh of relief when she recognized Gunner. He started talking as soon as she rolled down the window.

"We'd all appreciate it if you let us know when you have some news about Ned. Also, do what you can to make that guy get some rest. He's held up better than any of us expected, but he needs to shut it down soon before he collapses. We can handle the rest of the day, the prep for tomorrow and lock up afterward. No one wants to see him come back anytime soon."

Titus grumbled, "I'm sitting right here, Gunner."

The other man scoffed. "Heck, I'm not telling her anything I haven't already said to your face at least three times today, so don't bother snarling at me. I quit being scared of you ten minutes after I started working for you and don't see any reason to start up again."

Moira did her best not to laugh, but that was funny. She wasn't the only one who saw Titus for who he really was. Even when he'd claimed she'd already wasted too much time on him, he was trying to protect her from what he saw as his own failures. They'd talk about that later. For now, they had more pressing matters. "If we get any news about Ned, we'll let you know. I'll also keep an eye on Titus for you. I'm not scared of him, either."

Gunner laughed and stepped away from the SUV. "Do that."

He did an about-face and headed back into the café, where Rita was waiting for him. As

Moira eased the vehicle down the alley back toward the main road, she said, "It's nice of your staff to pick up the slack for you, but I can't say that I'm surprised. You've done the same for them."

"Yeah, yeah, I'm a real charmer." He crossed his arms over his chest and glared at her. "Now tell me what's going on. Where are you taking me?"

"We're heading for your house. TJ noticed something odd when he was out on patrol and asked me to come take a look. I did a drive-by and then called you. I want you to see it with fresh eyes, and then we'll talk."

Titus looked like he might explode at any second. The combination of no sleep and worry had taken its toll on him. She hadn't gotten much more sleep that he had, but at least her best friend hadn't gone missing. In short order, she turned into his driveway and parked. "Tell me if anything has changed since you left for work this morning."

Titus made no immediate effort to get out of the SUV. Instead, he leaned forward toward the windshield, as if those few inches made all the difference in how well he could see his house. After a second, Titus frowned.

"What's that stuck on the front door? An ad of some kind?"

She had her suspicions as to what it was, but she wasn't ready to jump to any conclusions. "So whatever it is wasn't there the last time you were here?"

"No, at least I'm pretty sure it wasn't." He leaned back in the seat again and frowned. "Although to be honest, I can't swear to that. I left in a hurry to start putting up notices about Ned."

No surprise there. "So here's the thing, Titus. I asked TJ to drive by a few times on his shift in case Ned came back and was sleeping on the front porch. TJ said he was pretty sure someone stuck that up there between the last two times he passed by your place. Our best guess is that it's been there no more than an hour and a half. Let's go check it out."

Moira half expected Titus to take off running, but he waited so they could approach the porch together. When they reached the steps, she stopped to snap a few pictures with her cell phone. After that, she pulled two pairs of gloves out of her pocket and offered a set to Titus. "It's not likely we'll get any forensic help from the county lab, but I'd still prefer to avoid contaminating any evidence."

She pointed toward the plastic bag taped to his front door. "You already know about the recent uptick in missing pets. A couple eventually came back of their own accord, but there have been several instances of a ransom demand for return of the animals. I probably should've thought about that being a possibility when you first said Ned had gone missing, but he doesn't exactly fit the profile of the other victims. They've all been cats or else small dogs. I couldn't imagine any stranger would try to dognap an animal the size of Ned. I'm sorry I didn't tell you sooner."

"No problem. I can see why you felt that way. Most people are a bit reluctant to approach Ned when they first meet him. There are a few adults he took to immediately, but he doesn't always go out of his way to make friends. Well, except when it comes to kids or people like your grandmother."

Those same things could be said of the dog's owner, too. The man and the dog were definitely kindred spirits. Meanwhile, Moira watched as Titus pulled on the gloves before reaching for the zip-top plastic bag. Using care, he peeled off the tape and then gently opened the bag, pausing several times to let her take more pictures. Finally, he removed the single sheet of paper from inside and set the plastic bag on the porch railing. Drawing a deep breath, he slowly unfolded the note and held the paper so they could both read it at the same time. The note was written in a shaky hand, but the message was clear. Titus needed to pony up some cash to get Ned back. Just like with the other incidents, he was supposed to stuff it in an unlabeled envelope and leave it in the phone booth next to the vacant gas station outside town.

He glared at the paper as if he couldn't believe his eyes. After folding it up again, he stuffed the note back in the plastic bag and handed it to her. "Seriously, whoever took him is asking for just sixty dollars to give him back? I'm insulted on Ned's behalf."

This wasn't a laughing matter, but Moira couldn't help herself. "Sorry, but you're not the first person to have that reaction. One of the earlier victims was a purebred champion with a ton of trophies and blue ribbons. His owner was furious that anyone would ask so little for the return of his pride and joy."

Titus looked incredulous, but Moira simply nodded. "It looks as if whoever is doing this operates on a sliding scale, maybe based on the size of the hostage. The demands I know about have been between twenty and thirty dollars, but Ned is two or three times bigger than any of the other animals, at least the ones that were brought to my attention."

His dark eyes looked haunted. "But they were returned unharmed?"

At least she could reassure him on that account. "Not only that, they appeared to have been well-fed. They'd also been bathed, and their coats brushed."

That information must have been the tipping point for Titus's ability to deal with the situation, because he grabbed for the porch rail and held on while he dropped down to sit on the porch steps. He braced his elbows on his knees and rested his face in his hands. "So you think I'll get Ned back."

Moira sat next to him and gently rested her arm across his back. "No guarantees, but based on the previous cases, I'd say it looks promising. After the first two people paid the ransoms, their pets reappeared early the next morning. No one saw anything. They just woke up to find their pets back home. They were even tethered to the front porch to make sure they didn't wander off."

Titus didn't say anything for the longest time. When he finally lifted his head to look around, his coloring had improved even if his hands were still shaky. "I've been scared sick that he'd either been hit by a car or else someone grabbed him to use in a dog-fighting ring."

He slowly rose to his feet, once again holding on to the porch rail for balance. "I'll get an envelope from inside and then hit the ATM for some cash. I could take it out of the till at the café, but I don't want anyone to know what's going on."

"Good thinking. Come on, I'll give you a ride."

He shook his head. "I appreciate the offer, but it's probably better that I'm not seen with you anywhere close to the drop-off location. If the kidnapper is watching, it could set off alarms if he or she thinks I've involved the police."

She rested her hand on his sleeve. "Are you sure you should be driving?"

He jerked his arm away from her. "I can handle it. Don't fuss over me."

Okay, that was enough. She growled right back at him. "Don't get all defensive, Titus. It's my job to worry about the safety of all of the citizens in Dunbar. It's my professional opinion that you should not be out driving right now. If something bad happened, you'd never forgive yourself."

To soften the moment, she added one more bit of truth. "And I can't stand the thought of you getting hurt. Let me call Max for you."

After a second, he sat back down. "Tell him to hurry."

"I will."

She stepped away to call both the office and then Max to explain the situation. It was a huge relief that he was home and available. "I'll tell him you're on the way. Thanks for doing this for him."

After hanging up, she returned to the porch and sat down again. It was time for her to head back to the station, but she didn't want to leave Titus alone. Max had promised to be on his way in matter of minutes. While they waited for him, she shared her own frustration. "I need to put an end to this situation before Cade gets back. He went to bat for me before he left, and I'd hate to disappoint him. He shouldn't have to come back to a bunch of angry citizens complaining because I couldn't figure out who was stealing their cats and dogs, especially for what's essentially chump change. Seriously, how weird is that?"

Titus shook his head. "It is a weird way to pick up some extra cash. In dribbles and drabs instead of one big money grab."

He was right. "I'd been wondering if the low ransoms were because it was kids doing this. Depending on their age, it might have seemed like a lot of money to them. Certainly their parents wouldn't be as likely to question them having a small amount of extra cash."

But the more she thought about it, that didn't make sense. Where would kids stash their captives without getting caught? There was another possibility. "But maybe this could be someone who desperately needs a small influx of cash."

"That makes more sense than anything I can think of right now." He nudged her shoulder with his. "Although I'm not at my sharpest right now. The question is what are we going to do about it? I don't want anyone else to go through the same scare about their pet as I have."

Moira mulled it over for a few seconds. "I hate to admit it, but I agree it's better not to have any kind of police presence near the drop-off. There's no telling what would happen if we were spotted and panicked the culprit when they come for the ransom. Too bad the drop isn't someplace with security cameras. If we had more time, maybe we could borrow some equipment from the county sheriff's office, or maybe find one of those motion-activated cameras that hunters use to track animals."

Titus sat up straighter. "I'll ask Max to give me a ride up to Leavenworth. We should be able to buy one of those there."

"Save the receipt in case I can put it on my expense account."

"No, Ned's my responsibility."

It was tempting to argue the point, but she knew stubborn when she saw it. With neither of them operating at peak capacity, it was simpler to let Titus have his way for now. She could always bring up the subject when Cade returned to see what he thought.

"I'm guessing you and Max can handle the installation."

"Can't be all that hard. He may even know something about how they work. I'm betting he's done a few freelance articles on wildlife photography at some point."

There wasn't much more to say on the matter. She could only hope for Titus's sake that Ned showed up on his doorstep soon. The man wouldn't find any peace until that happened. "Promise me after you install the camera and drop off the money, you'll try to get some sleep. I have another hour on my shift, and I'm counting the minutes until I can go home and pull the covers up over my head."

For an instant it seemed like he wouldn't respond, but he finally did. "I can't promise I'll sleep, but I will stay home and zone out in front of the television. Since Gunner is doing the prep, I don't need to go into work until tomorrow."

She'd take what she could get. To pass the time, she took advantage of the moment to do something she'd been wanting to do for a while now. Leaning in closer, she studied the swirl of tattoos on his closest arm. After a bit, she frowned. What had originally looked like a geometric pattern now appeared to be highly stylized letters. Cocking her head to the side, she tried to make sense of them. After a bit, she poked the first letter. "Okay, I give up. What does that say?"

He twisted his arm to give her a better look. "That's my grandmother's name. She's the one who took me in after I ran away from my mother and stepfather. I lived with her until I left for college. There's no telling where I would have ended up without her in my life. I had it done not long after she passed away."

There was a lot to unpack in those few words, leaving her with so many questions about his past. Now wasn't the time. "Do you have other names hidden in among all that artwork?"

He pointed out another spot. "That's the emblem for my father's unit with his name and rank written below it. Dad was killed while serving in the army when I was in my early teens."

Well, rats. What she'd hoped would be an innocent distraction to pass the time while they waited for Max was turning out to be a disaster. "I'm so sorry."

"Me, too. He was a great guy, and I miss

him every day. I always wonder what he would think of some of my life choices. For one thing, I'm the first in four generations not to serve in the military."

She knew the answer to that one. "If he was anything like you, he'd be proud that you were a good cop and sacrificed a lot trying to bring down a drug ring. He'd also be glad you found a career that makes you genuinely happy and that you have so many friends who care about you. Just so you know, I also got an earful about you at the game while you were umpiring. Seems you do a lot for the people here in town. When help is needed, they all said you step up without asking for anything in return."

She glanced up at him to see how he was reacting to her assessment of his life. "Why, Titus Kondrat, I do believe you're blushing."

The look of disgust he gave her had her holding up her hands. "Your secret is safe with me. If anyone asks, I'll deny to my dying breath that you're a nice guy underneath all those tats and bad attitude."

To hide her grin, she turned her attention back to his tattoos. A ripple of shock rolled through her when she recognized one final name written on a small heart tucked in be-tween the stems of two beautiful roses. She said the letters aloud as she traced them with her finger. *"M-o-i-r-a."*

She dragged her gaze up to meet his. "You have my name on your arm."

The corner of his mouth quirked up in a small smile. "I do."

"Why would you do that, Titus? More importantly, when did you do that?"

He caught her hand in his and held it. "When I got out of the hospital, I had a lot of time on my hands while I went through all the physical therapy and other rehab I needed. I somehow found myself getting inked. Once I started, I decided I didn't just want a bunch of meaningless artwork, so I had the artist add in the names of people, places and things that meant something to me. The first three names were the obvious ones—my grandmother's, my father's and yours. Ned's will be next."

A second later, he used the knuckle on his forefinger to lift her chin and close her mouth. There was a twinkle in his eyes that had been missing since his furry companion had disappeared. "What's the matter, Officer Fraser?

You're looking a bit frazzled there. Must be the lack of sleep."

Before she could frame a coherent question, a car pulled into the driveway. Titus jumped to his feet. "Well, that'll be my ride. I'll keep you posted about what happens."

Then he was gone, leaving her staring at his back.

CHAPTER TWENTY

TWELVE HOURS LATER, Titus shifted on his bed, trying without success to get more comfortable. He pointed the remote at the television and clicked through the channels, trying to find something that could hold his attention. He would've been happier sitting on the couch, but he didn't want to hang out in the living room for fear the kidnapper might be scared off by any sign of life inside the house.

It was half-past four in the morning, so his miserable night would finally end. The only question was what would happen between now and when the sun finally crested the horizon.

It had taken all the willpower Titus could muster to stay home instead of staking out the gas station to see if Ned's captor claimed the ransom. He kept reminding himself that he'd promised Moira he would stay home and get some rest. He'd given her his word, and he needed her to learn she could trust him if they were ever going to have any kind of future together. It also wasn't worth the risk of spooking the kidnapper. Who knew what would happen to Ned if Titus was spotted lurking in the shadows at the gas station.

He finally gave up in disgust and shut off the television. The silence settled around him, making him feel more alone than ever. His solitary life didn't used to bother him, but that had changed the day Ned moved in to stay. He still had no idea why the dog had chosen Titus to be his new owner out of all the other people in town, but he done his best to make sure Ned never had cause for regret. At the time, Titus hadn't been looking to adopt a pet of his own despite his volunteer work for the local shelters, but then he wasn't actually the one who made the final decision. He'd left that up to Ned.

Regardless, even Titus had to admit that it had done him a world of good to have someone who actually needed him. Yeah, the people he employed at the café depended on Titus for their income, but there were other jobs to be had. He liked them and considered their welfare with each decision he made regarding the café. That wasn't the same as having someone waiting at home every night who was happy to see him walk back through the door.

Titus might have started making connections with people right after he moved to Dunbar, but the process had definitely sped up once he opened his home to Ned. It had been the first real move toward letting himself get close to others, to push past the barriers he'd built to hide behind.

The thought of going back to being that alone again... No, he wouldn't even think about that possibility. Besides, he had other friends now: Cade, Max, Gunner, Rita and Beth. And, God willing, he'd have Ned. And then there was Moira. Although he'd tried to warn her off, she kept coming back to help him. Maybe he hadn't screwed up as badly as he thought he had when it came to her. A man could only hope.

In the distance, he heard the chime that signaled he had a new text message. He rolled up to his feet to retrieve his phone, which was charging on the kitchen counter. He must have dozed off at some point, because he'd missed messages from both Max and Moira before this most recent one. He sent a quick response to Max, telling him he was hanging in there, but there was still no sign of Ned. He also thanked him again for helping to get the camera set up. After promising that he'd let him know if there was news, he moved on to Moira's two messages.

The first one had come in over an hour ago and was short and to the point. You doing okay?

The second was longer. Hey, checking in again. I hope you were able to catch some shut-eye, but figure that's not happening. Call if you want to talk. I'm up.

Should he? Why not? Moira wouldn't have made the offer if she hadn't meant it. He grabbed a can of pop out of the fridge and settled in at the table before making the call. It was a relief when she answered on the first ring.

"Any news?"

"Not so far. I'm scared to look out front for fear of…well, I'm not sure what, exactly." He stopped to take a calming breath before continuing. "I figure Ned will let me know when he gets home."

If he gets home.

He shoved that thought back down into the darkest depths of his mind. Time to change topics. "What are you doing up at this hour?"

Moira sighed. "Gram had a rough night. Sometimes she can't sleep and gets agitated. When that happens, one of us stays up to make sure she doesn't try to slip out of the house."

He could hear the near exhaustion in her voice. "I'm sorry. Is she doing better now?"

"I fixed her a cup of herbal tea and put one of her favorite old movies on to play. She dozed off in her recliner about an hour ago. It didn't seem like a good idea to wake her up just to send her to bed, so I covered her with a blanket and turned off the lights. I'm sitting in the kitchen killing time until Mom takes over so I can get ready for work."

"That's gotta be tough on all of you."

"Yeah, it is. But speaking of sleeping, were you able to get any rest?"

"No, but not for lack of trying. I've been hiding out in my bedroom to avoid being seen from the front of the house."

She chuckled. "Sounds like we're each doing a lot of skulking around in the dark tonight."

"It would be more fun if we were skulking around together. We should try it sometime."

"Maybe I'll give you a call the next time I have to do a stakeout."

Curiosity got the better of him, so he asked, "Does that happen a lot here in Dunbar? Because I'll bring the snacks."

"Sadly, not very often. But if you're going to bring some of your mini pies, I might just fake one."

His mind filled with the image of the two of them sitting alone in the dark and quietly talking for hours about anything and everything. Oh, yeah, he would be totally down with that. "Just name the time and the place."

"Oops, I'd better go. I think Mom is headed this way. Keep me posted on…well, you know."

Titus didn't want to hang up, but Moira's family needed her right now. With everything she had going on with her job and her grandmother, it was a wonder that she had enough energy left over for anyone else. Especially him, but he wasn't going to suggest that she stop.

"You'll be the first one I call. If…no, make that *when* Ned shows up, we'll have to retrieve the camera. I think it would be best if you or one of the other officers went with me to do that since it might have the evidence you need to put a stop to this. I'll sleep a lot better when the culprit is behind bars."

"We all will. What time do you have to leave for work? If Ned isn't back by then, I'll make sure to swing by your place periodically to check on things."

He didn't want to set foot out of the house until he got his roommate back, but he was needed at the café. "I'll have to leave by five thirty to help Gunner open up."

"Okay, we'll start doing drive-bys after that."

"Thanks, Moira. That's above and beyond, but I appreciate it."

Once they hung up, he checked the time. He needed to head for work in less than an hour. Before leaving the kitchen, he stopped long enough to fill Ned's bowl with fresh water and to put out some treats, just in case. Having done everything he could to prepare for his roommate's imminent return, he headed down the hall to shower and get dressed.

TITUS WAS IN no shape to be around anyone right now, but he had no choice. He'd barely found the strength to open his front door when it came time to leave for the café. His gut told him that if Ned had been returned, the dog would have made his presence known. Even knowing that, he'd been so hopeful that he would step out on the porch to find him sleeping in the bed Titus kept out there for him.

Seeing the bed empty had left Titus feeling physically ill. Instead of ducking back inside and slamming the door, he forced himself to head off to work like he would on any other day. It was tempting to ride the Harley, but he opted for the pickup, the safer option all things considered. Besides, he'd need it to retrieve the camera later since Max had made him promise to take him along for the ride.

The trip to the café was both too short and too long. He needed more time to prepare himself for the barrage of questions that would come flying his way about Ned's continued absence. But he also needed to get to the café, where he could lose himself in the routine of feeding people. It was unusual for him to beat Gunner to work, but the other man's rattletrap car was not in its usual spot across the street. At least that would give

Titus a chance to get inside and settle himself a bit.

But as he turned down the alley to park the truck, he slammed on the brakes and rubbed his eyes to make sure he wasn't seeing things. Realizing his eyes were working just fine, he jumped out of the truck and ran for the small porch at the back door of the café.

"Ned!"

The dog was tied to the railing of the steps. He'd been lying down, but he lurched to his feet, barking and wagging his tail like crazy. Titus sat down on the steps and gathered his friend in close, burying his face in the dog's silky fur. It took a few seconds to be able to believe that Ned was back, safe and sound.

Titus unfastened the rope that had been used to tie Ned to the railing. "Come on, boy, let's go inside."

As soon as the door opened, Ned shoved past Titus to sniff his way around the kitchen, maybe wanting to make sure that nothing had changed in the short time he'd been away. When he reached his bed, he sat down on the cushion with an expectant look on his face. Titus wasn't about to deny the dog anything he might want. "I'll get you some treats, boy."

After grabbing a handful out of the jar, Titus leaned against the wall and slid down to sit next to the basket. Still waiting for his pulse to return to some approximation of normal, he fed Ned a treat and then texted Max to tell him the good news. He followed that up with a quick message to Moira. He'd just sent it when Gunner arrived. As soon as he spotted Ned, he grinned and headed straight for him. "I see you came back, you worthless mooch. Don't think I'm going to be slipping you bits of bacon after the scare you put us through. Not to mention what a pain in the backside your owner has been about the whole affair. What kind of friend are you to go wandering off like that?"

Titus reached over to give his buddy a thorough scratching. "It wasn't his fault. Ned was kidnapped. I paid the ransom last night."

Gunner stepped back in shock. "Seriously? Who would do something like that?"

As Titus explained the situation, the door opened and closed again as Moira joined the welcome-home party. He left it up to her to respond to Gunner's question. "We don't know yet, but I'm going to do everything I can to make sure they don't do it again."

She kneeled by Titus's side. "How is he?"

"Fine, near as I can tell." Titus leaned in close to take another sniff of Ned's fur. "For one thing, he's had a bath."

Clearly puzzled, Gunner asked, "How can you tell that?"

"It's a different scent than the shampoo I use on him. He's also had his nails trimmed."

By that point, Gunner was frowning in disbelief. "So you want me to believe Ned was kidnapped and held prisoner at a doggy spa?"

Moira stood. "Actually, the same thing happened to some other animals who've gone missing lately."

"Well, that's just plain weird, even for Dunbar."

"You'll get no argument from me on that point." Titus pushed himself back up to his feet. "I hope it's okay, but Max wants to go with us to retrieve the camera. He should be here any second now. I need to get back to help with the early morning rush. Do you have time to go with us now?"

"Yeah, I told Oscar what was going on. He'll cover for me."

"Then we should go now."

Ned beat them both to the door. Titus didn't

even try to convince him to stay with Gunner. After clipping on Ned's leash, he let the dog lead the charge back outside. Just as promised, Max came jogging around the corner. Ned barked a greeting and allowed yet another one of his human friends to praise him for returning home. Afterward, the four of them piled into Moira's SUV and headed for the drop site.

The parking lot was empty with no one else in sight when they arrived. It was no surprise that the envelope that had contained the ransom was long gone. Once again, Moira took pictures of everything, including the camera they'd mounted on a nearby tree. When she was satisfied that she had everything documented, she passed out gloves. After putting them on, Max carefully removed the camera and handed it over to Moira.

Titus explained the setup on the camera. "We had it set to take a quick series of photos and then a short video whenever it was activated."

The three of them stood close together as they checked out the pictures. The first set caught a coyote on the hunt. Moira skipped through those pictures and video to get to the next one. It showed a trio of deer making their way from the trees on the other side of the road to the open field behind the station. Interesting, but not helpful.

"There's one more to go."

Titus tamped down his growing anger as he waited for her to push the button. If they failed to learn the identity of the kidnapper, someone else in town would likely go through the same pain and fear that he had.

Max grinned as he pointed to the screen. "We got a human this time."

Yeah, they had, but it was impossible to tell if it was a man or a woman in the first photo. Whoever it was had come dressed in dark pants and a sweatshirt with the hood cinched down tight to hide his or her face and hair.

The second picture wasn't much better, but the third time was the charm. After studying the last photo for several seconds, Moira held the camera so that all three of them could watch the video. After watching it once, she played it again as if having a hard time believing what her eyes were telling her.

When it was finished, Max pointed to the figure on the screen. "I'm guessing you both recognize that person, but I don't. Who is it?"

Titus gave him an honest answer. "No one I would have expected to see."

Moira nodded, looking grim. "But we're definitely going to go see her now."

CHAPTER TWENTY-ONE

MOIRA WASN'T SURE she should have allowed Titus to come with her, but it would've been a major fight to get him to wait at the café to find out what she learned. Titus wasn't the only one who had insisted on coming along for the ride. When they'd tried to leave Ned at the café, the dog had dug in his paws and refused to leave Titus's side. In the end, he'd ridden in her back seat with his nose stuck out the window, happily sniffing the wind.

While Moira could play hardball with the best of them, she couldn't bring herself to separate the pair right now. She was pretty sure it would be a long while before Titus let Ned out of his sight for any length of time. Besides, she was a firm believer that a victim had some rights. Both Titus and Ned deserved their chance to confront the woman who had put them through the wringer over the past two days. The dollar amounts in the kidnappings didn't add up to a huge amount, but the pet owners had paid a high price in worry and fear.

Once they reached their destination, Moira parked her cruiser on the street and led the parade up the driveway. Before stepping onto the porch, she laid out some ground rules for her companion. "I'll do all the talking, Titus. It's my job."

"I know."

She pressed the doorbell and then stepped back as she called out, "We're here on official police business. Please open the door."

The curtain on the front window twitched as if someone had peeked out, but then it fell back into place. When there was no further response, Moira raised her hand and knocked on the door, putting considerable oomph into her effort to show she meant business.

Finally, there was the click of the lock being turned, and the door opened just a crack. "I'm sorry, Moira, but I'm not entertaining visitors right now. Perhaps if you could come back later this afternoon."

When the door started to close again, Moira blocked it. "I'm sorry, Mrs. Redd, but that's not going to happen. I'm here investigating a series of crimes, and I have reason to believe that you are involved."

The older woman gasped. "Moira Fraser, your mother and grandmother will both be horrified to learn how rude you're being to me."

Titus had been standing off to the side, but he'd obviously heard enough. When he took a step closer, Moira maneuvered so she remained between him and Mrs. Redd. "I wouldn't be here if I didn't have hard evidence that you kidnapped Mr. Kondrat's dog. In fact, it's a slam dunk that you're behind the recent crime spree of missing pets."

Calling it a crime spree was a bit of a stretch, But at least she'd managed to get through to the woman. Mrs. Redd opened the door wide and stared at Moira and her two companions. Ned whined and wagged his tail, as if happy to see the older woman, another indication that she'd treated her captives well.

After a second, Mrs. Redd seemed to shrink in on herself. "You'd better come inside."

Moira followed her mother's friend down the hall and into the living room. Titus followed close behind with Ned by his side. Their unwilling hostess motioned toward the sofa and chair. "Have a seat. Can I offer you any refreshments?"

Titus took one end of the sofa while Moira took the other. Ned jumped up on the middle cushion and lay down. Stroking the dog's head, Titus grumbled, "We're here for explanations, not to be entertained."

He was right about that and had every right to be angry. Regardless, they'd get more from the woman if they kept the conversation civil. Moira gave him a reproachful look and then turned her attention to Mrs. Redd. "What we need is an explanation about what's going on in your life to make you do something like this. You're not the kind of person who would turn to a life of crime for no reason."

The older woman sank down on the chair, her face pale. Her hands trembled as she looked everywhere but at her guests. When she spoke, her voice was a mere whisper. "I live on a limited income. As long as nothing unexpected happens, I do okay."

Ned sat back up and stared at her. Before Titus could stop him, he hopped down off the sofa, sat next to her feet and leaned against her legs. Mrs. Redd stroked his fur with a soft smile on her face. "You're such a good boy, Ned."

Turning her attention to Titus, she bit her lower lip before speaking. "I'm sorry, Mr. Kondrat. You're such a polite young man, and you're always so generous with your customers. I often get an extra dinner and sometimes even another lunch out of those delicious meals I order at the café. Regardless, I should never have taken Ned home with me. You must have been worried sick about him. Neither of you deserved that."

Moira wouldn't have been surprised if Titus snarled at the woman again, but she should have known better. Like his dog, the man had a soft spot for people who were in pain. He leaned back and released a long, slow breath. "Just tell us what's going on."

Mrs. Redd sounded so tired when she finally came clean. "If it had been only one unexpected expense, I would have been all right. But this house is getting old, and I had several big repair bills all at once. I've been keeping up on the payments, but I admit that it's been a struggle. Then my doctor put me on a medicine that's very expensive. I don't have to take it forever, but it's still more than I can afford on top of everything else."

She kept stroking Ned's head. "I honestly don't know why I thought holding pets hostage was a good idea. I was bound to get caught eventually, but I kept telling myself I'd stop after one more. That somehow I'd find another way to get the money."

Mrs. Redd stopped to stare at the small diamond ring on her hand. "The alternative would've been to sell my wedding ring, but that would've been like losing my husband all over again."

The woman's story made Moira's heart hurt. Now what was she supposed to do? If she actually arrested Mrs. Redd, that would only add to her financial woes. "Do you have any other pets visiting with you right now?"

"Oh, no. Ned was the last one." She sat with her shoulders hunched, making her look older and more fragile than she actually was. "I'd already made up my mind to stop."

Moira believed her. "That's a step in the right direction."

"I know it doesn't change anything, but I took good care of the animals while they were with me."

"I could tell." Titus looked down at Ned. "I don't know what you used on his coat, but it feels softer and looks shinier than what I've been using."

His comment triggered an interesting idea. Moira mentally poked and prodded it for a few seconds as she considered all the possible ramifications. She wasn't sure what the mayor and city council would think, but she decided to give it a shot.

"Mrs. Redd, we both know there will have to be consequences for what you've done. So here's my thought. Have you ever considered earning some extra money grooming animals for your friends and neighbors? You obviously have a talent for it. Or maybe boarding a dog or cat if their owners need to be out of town occasionally?"

The older woman sat up a little straighter. "I hadn't, but I actually enjoyed taking care of my…guests. They were good company."

"I can't make any promises because I don't have the authority to make this decision. However, I'm willing to make the suggestion if you're interested. Of course, you might have to do it for free for the owners of your guests. It would be like doing community service to make up for what you've done."

Explaining all of this to her boss might prove interesting, but she suspected that Cade would likely be grateful for a solution to the problem. No one would want to see Mrs. Redd behind bars.

By that point, Titus was looking marginally happier. "Officer Fraser, I can write a letter to Mayor Klaus and the city council in support of the plan if that would help."

Moira smiled first at him and then at Mrs. Redd. "I'll make some calls and let you know."

THE NEXT EVENING, Moira picked up the pizza for the girls' movie night that she had promised to spend with Carli. They'd immediately settled on opposite ends of the couch to watch the rom-com Carli had chosen. Sadly, less than half an hour in, Moira had already lost track of the plot and all interest in the pizza.

"Where are you tonight?"

Moira dragged her eyes away from the television to see what Carli was talking about. After all, the answer was pretty obvious.

"I'm here with you. Remember you invited me over for pizza and a movie."

"I know I did, but it doesn't feel as if you're here at all. I'm not complaining. I'm worried. Something is bothering you. Does it have to do with Mrs. Redd and what she did? I thought you'd worked something out with the mayor and the city council."

"I did. In fact, they were thrilled with the solution I came up with. Otto was even making noise about writing up an official commendation for my record. We need to wait until Cade gets back to make it all official."

"That's great, but something definitely has you all tied up in knots."

Feeling a bit defensive, Moira frowned at her friend. "What makes you think that?"

Carli shifted to face Moira directly as she started counting off her reasons for concern. "First, you've barely spoken a word all evening. Second, since when do you only eat a single slice of pizza? Seriously, it's not like you to let all that delicious pepperoni go to waste."

Then she pointed toward the glass of wine on the coffee table. "And you've barely touched your drink. I bought that bottle specifically because it's one of your favorites. Add all that up, and it's pretty clear that at least your head is somewhere else."

Her friend wasn't wrong, but Moira still tried to deny it. "I don't know what you're talking about."

"Yes, you do." Carli narrowed her eyes as she pointed at Moira. "If I were a gambler, I'd bet all of my money that whatever has you all tied up in knots has to do with Titus Kondrat."

Moira winced at her friend's accurate summation of the situation. "I'm sorry. I'll do better."

Carli turned off the television. "I don't want you to pretend you're enjoying yourself. I want to know what's wrong. Do I actually need to borrow a bat and go have a talk with that man? Because I will."

Okay, that image never got less funny. "No, that won't be necessary. I'm not upset with Titus. It's more that I don't know what to do about him."

"Why not?"

"He's not who I thought he was." She reached for her wineglass and took a big swig. "No, that's not right. It's more that he's not who he used to be."

Her friend sipped her own wine, shaking her head. "Honey, if you think that was any clearer, you're sadly mistaken. Try again."

"I'm saying it's who Titus used to be that is the problem." Maybe it was time to lay it all out there for Carli. "Promise me that what I'm about to tell you won't go any further. There are reasons why Titus is closemouthed about his past. Good ones. But if I don't tell you some of it, none of this will make sense."

Looking solemn and not a little confused, Carli held up her hand. "Consider me sworn to silence."

"Okay then. Here's the thing. Titus is Ryan. Well, he never really was Ryan at all, but I didn't know that back then. I do now."

Carli sat up taller, her eyes wide with disbelief. "I never met Ryan, but you told me a lot about him. That he was charming, a fancy dresser and a fast talker. What is it about Titus that could possibly remind you of that jerk?"

"That's just it. Titus doesn't just remind me of Ryan. He is…no, he actually *was* Ryan Donovan ten years ago, when I knew him. It was the name Titus used when he was an undercover cop. That's all I can tell you about that time in his life. The truth is that Titus was never arrested or sent to prison, but a bunch of things happened afterward that were out of his control. For his safety and mine, he had to stay away."

"So you're saying when you were dating Ryan, you were actually dating Titus even though you didn't know it."

When Moira nodded, Carli frowned. "And somehow ten years later he magically ended up living in your hometown. How come you didn't recognize him as soon as you saw him?"

"I might have figured it out sooner, but I think he used to avoid letting me get anywhere close to him. For sure, he did look vaguely familiar, but part of what I can't tell you altered his appearance permanently. Also, when he was Ryan, Titus's hair was almost blond, he wore blue contact lenses and he was built along leaner lines. More like a swimmer. His wardrobe was also much more upscale."

Carli held up her hand as if she needed a second to absorb that much information. Finally, she said, "And now he has dark hair, brown eyes, is totally ripped and has a huge collection of flannel shirts."

"Yep, and the tats are a new addition, too." Moira leaned forward and whispered, "He has my name inked on his left arm. It's on a small heart between two roses."

"Wow, that's a lot to take in." Carli blinked several times and then said, "I'm guessing it's no accident that he opened a café here in Dunbar."

"Nope. He figured if he moved here, we would cross paths eventually."

"What was he hoping would happen? I mean, if all he wanted was forgiveness, he could've reached out years ago. More importantly, now that you know the truth, what do you hope will happen? Because that's the real question."

"Yeah, it is. Even though what Ryan and I had seemed so special, it wasn't built on anything real." Moira set her glass back on the coffee table. "Since I moved back to Dunbar, I've gotten to know Titus better than I ever really knew Ryan. He's a good man, and he has no problem with me being a cop. That's more than the last guy I seriously dated could claim."

She swiped a stray tear from her cheek. "My heart wants to give us another chance, but he recently told me I shouldn't waste more of my time on him. He was upset about Ned disappearing when he said it, but what if he really meant it?"

Her friend's expression turned sympathetic. "But what if he didn't, Moira? You said yourself he was hurting at the time."

"We're not the same people we were ten years ago."

"No, you're not, but maybe that's not a bad thing. How do you feel about this version of Titus? And how does he feel about you?"

Moira closed her eyes and let images of Titus flood into her mind. Him high-fiving kids at the ball game. The gentle kindness he'd shown both her grandmother and Mrs. Redd. The way he showed up with food whenever there was trouble. And how right it felt when he kissed her.

"I like him, more than I ever thought possible." As soon as she admitted that much, she knew *like* wasn't a strong enough word for how she felt about him. But if she was going to find the courage to admit that she actually loved Titus, he deserved to be the first to know. "I think he feels the same, too."

At least she hoped so.

Carli stood and offered Moira a hand up off the couch. "As much as I normally enjoy your company, you're not going to find answers sitting here with me. You're a smart woman and know what you've got to do."

Yeah, she did. "You're the best friend ever."

"I know. Now, pack up the rest of the pizza, go find the man and see what happens."

Moira did as ordered. Before heading for the door, she gave Carli a quick hug. "This is crazy."

"Just know that I'm rooting for you. If you two can find something special despite everything you've been through, then maybe there's hope for me, too."

NED WOOFED AND stared out the front window. Titus was already up and moving before the doorbell rang. He'd been half expecting Max to show up wanting to learn the full story behind Ned's capture, but it definitely wasn't him standing on the porch looking shy and not at all sure of her welcome.

Titus stood back out of the way. "Moira, this is a nice surprise. Come on in."

She held out the pizza box in her hand. "I thought this might go with that bottle of Malbec I gave you."

He lifted the lid, noting there were two pieces missing. "Did you get a discount because someone else ate part of it?"

She blushed. "Actually, I'm supposed to be over at Carli's watching a movie and sharing a bottle of pinot grigio."

"And yet here you are with me."

"I am."

She remained close to the door as if she had doubts about whether she wanted to stay at all. He had to do something to get her to hang around long enough to find out why she had deserted her best friend and headed for his place. Rather than peppering her with questions, he fell back on his default setting.

"While I could reheat the pizza, I actually have something better that's ready to serve. Besides, I told you I'd save the Malbec for when you'd let me cook dinner for you. This might be more spontaneous than I expected, but you'll love my saltimbocca."

"Sounds fancy."

Laughing, he headed for the kitchen and hoped she'd follow. "It's just chicken cutlets with mushrooms, prosciutto and cheese in a wine sauce."

To give her something to focus on, he pointed at a cabinet and then at a drawer. "Why don't you set the table while I put the finishing touches on dinner?"

She made quick work of her assigned duty. When she'd arranged everything to her satisfaction, she stood next to him at the stove. "That smells delicious. I'm glad you made extra."

"Me, too."

He tasted the sauce and added a touch more salt. "It needs to simmer another minute or two to thicken. Keep an eye on it for me while I open the wine."

When he served their meal, she hesitated before picking up her fork, looking a little panicky. "Moira, eat. We can talk about whatever brought you here afterward."

She rolled her shoulders as if trying to shed some of her tension. It must have worked because they were able to carry on a casual conversation for the duration of the meal. When he cleared away their empty plates, he said,

"I'm sorry, but I don't have any dessert to offer you."

Staring at him in mock horror, her hand on her chest, she gasped, "You mean you don't keep chocolate-cream pie on hand on the off chance that I'll show up at the door with a half-eaten pizza?"

He topped off their wineglasses. "I will from now on if it means you'll do this again soon."

And just that quickly, all of her tension came roaring back. "About that—I thought we should talk."

"Okay, but let's take this discussion to the couch."

"Shouldn't we do the dishes first?"

"No, they can wait. I'm not sure whatever you need to talk about can."

He tugged her up from her chair. "Come on, and bring the wine. I suspect we might need it."

Ned was zoned out on the couch, taking up more than his fair share of space. "Move it, dog."

Most of the time, Ned would have either ignored the order or else taken his own sweet time moving out of Titus's way. Maybe he sensed something serious was afoot, because he immediately vacated his spot and headed for his fallback position on the chair. Titus sat down in his own usual spot and then tumbled Moira down next to him. He held her there with his arm around her shoulders before she could put any distance between them.

If she'd fought to get away, he would've let her go. When she settled in closer after only a few seconds, he gave her a nudge. "So tell me what's going on. Why did you abandon Carli to show up on my doorstep?"

"I had questions, ones she couldn't answer, not even when I told her you were Ryan." Moira swallowed hard and met his gaze with worried eyes. "I swore her to secrecy."

He didn't know where this conversation was headed, but at least he could reassure her on that much. "It's fine, Moira. My past is bound to come out eventually. I already told Max some of it, and I plan to tell Cade when he gets back. Since neither man likes keeping secrets from their wives, that probably means Shelby and Rikki are both going to find out soon as well."

She looked relieved. "Anyway, Carli already knew about me and Ryan...you, that is. She saw how hard it was for me to get over you. Looking back, I should have recognized the signs that something wasn't right. I'm not sure if I was incredibly naive or willfully blind."

Interesting. "What kind of signs?"

"We were together for two months, and I didn't have a single picture of you. The fact that I never met any of your friends. You never talked about your family." She waved her hand in the air. "None of that matters now. The point is that I trusted you, and we both know how that turned out."

Titus struggled to draw a full breath, all the pain from that time in his life bearing down hard on him. "I hate that I hurt you. I never meant for that to happen."

Moira twisted to look up at him. "If I mattered back then, why didn't you find a way to tell me the truth?"

"Because I was a coward."

She immediately scoffed at that idea. "How do you figure? Cowards don't live a year undercover knowing every minute that something could go fatally wrong. That takes nerves of steel."

He huffed a bitter laugh. "Risking my own

life wasn't scary, but knowing I could be putting you at risk if Cian Henshaw or his people found out about you was terrifying. There was also the fact that you were in love with the very flashy Ryan Donovan. What if you didn't feel the same way about plain old Titus Kondrat?"

He liked that she didn't immediately dismiss what he was telling her. Finally, she threaded her fingers through his, holding his hand in her lap. "So what changed, Titus? It's been a long time since all of that blew up in our faces. You could've tracked me down long before now. Instead, after all this time, you moved here and waited to see if I'd ever show up. How long did you plan to stay in Dunbar, especially if I never moved back?"

The woman had a talent for asking the hard questions. "Honestly, I didn't think that far ahead. Early on, I focused on getting the café up and running. I was lucky that Gunner wanted his old job back and that Rita and Beth were looking for work. Once we opened, I made sure I stayed too busy to have time to think much past the next week's menu."

Ned raised his head to give Titus a long look. He got down from the chair, stretched and then circled around the coffee table to lay his head on Titus's knee. The familiar connection made it easier to keep talking. "Things started to change when this fur ball first showed up. I hadn't had anyone in my life who belonged to me since my grandmother passed. Once Ned claimed me as his owner, somehow Dunbar became my home, not just a place to hang out until the real part of my life would finally begin."

It was time to throw the dice and see what happened. He muscled Moira up from where she was sitting to settle her on his lap. It meant a lot that she didn't resist, and even more when she cuddled against his chest. "That last part happened the day you moved back to town."

"Why didn't you say something when I first got here?"

"Didn't you hear me when I said I was a coward? Besides that, you deserved time to settle in. You were dealing with a new job and your grandmother's issues. The last thing you needed was me showing up on your doorstep."

She pondered that for a few seconds before finally nodding. "When I first came back, I secretly thought it would only be a temporary move. You know, we'd get Gram situated somewhere safe, and then I could go back to Seattle and get my old life back."

"And now?"

Because if that's what she wanted, he'd have to let her go even if it would almost destroy him. She leaned in closer to tuck her head under his chin. "You're not the only one who has realized how special Dunbar is. I like being so close to my family and friends. I'm also happier working for a small police force. Helping and protecting people I actually know is surprisingly satisfying. I would miss all of those things if I moved back to Seattle."

Then she cupped his cheek with her hand. "Most of all I would miss you. You're not the man I knew back then, but I'm not the same woman, either. Carli is a smart lady. She asked how I felt about the man you are now."

"And what did you tell her?"

"I said that I liked you, but that was an understatement." She offered him an uncertain smile. "What I feel for you is way more than that. I'm pretty sure that I've fallen in love with the real you, and I thought you should be the first one to hear me say those words."

It was everything he'd hoped for and way too terrifying to believe. He covered her hand with his. "Considering all the bad things you suspected me of, when did this surprising change of heart happen?"

Her cheeks flushed pink. "First, I should apologize for some of the things I said, but I think I was running scared. I haven't been this attracted to a man in a long, long time."

He waved that off. "You have solid instincts, Moira. That's what makes you such a great cop. They were screaming that something about me didn't add up right. Don't forget that I could have saved both of us trouble if I had told you sooner that Ryder and I were helping out the local animal shelters."

"True, but I still shouldn't have jumped to the worst conclusion possible."

He smiled down at her. "Let's call it a draw as to which of us was in the wrong."

"It's a deal. And so, back to your question— I think it was when I realized how often you take care of people. It's the way you show up with food whenever something is going on, and how you're always so gentle with my grandmother. You offered Max a safe harbor in the café back when half the people in town hated him and stepped up to help him and Cade end the threat to Rikki and her son. And most of all, you trust me to be able to handle whatever my job throws at me even though it goes against your protective nature. That last one is huge."

Moira paused to kiss his cheek. "The list goes on, but all of those things define who you are—the man I love."

His heart felt lighter than it had in years. Maybe ever. "That's good, because I love you, too. Always have, always will."

Then he kissed her, taking his time to make sure this woman knew just how amazing she was. Learning that she loved him felt as if all the broken pieces of his life had suddenly snapped back together. The two of them sat in silence, maybe needing a little time to come to terms with the abrupt change in their relationship. When she finally stirred, he tightened his hold on her.

"Before I let go, I have two questions for you."

She settled back in. "Okay. Ask away."

Feeling as if he was about to step off the

high dive without knowing how deep the water was below, he asked, "I might be moving too fast, but I have to know—are you going marry me? Because I want it all—you, me, Ned, maybe even a couple of kids."

There was a quick intake of breath, and then she nodded without speaking. "Sorry, Moira, but I need to hear you say the words."

She pushed away from his chest to look him straight in the eyes. "Yes, Titus Kondrat, I'm going to marry you."

The determination in her words meant everything. The second question had more to do with logistics. "Now that we have that much settled, I have to know one more thing. Can we elope like Max and Rikki did, or are you going to make me jump through the kind of hoops that Shelby put Cade through?"

That had her laughing. "I don't want or need all those fancy bells and whistles. We'll keep things simple. You know, a few friends, my mom and Gram. I'm thinking Carli and Shelby should be my bridesmaids. Max and Cade can be their escorts."

Then she reached down to pet Ned. "And your buddy here will be our ring bearer."

He could deal with that. "Perfect."

She sighed contentedly. "It will be."

So this was what real happiness felt like. Before he could share that thought with Moira, she asked a couple of questions of her own. "Can I have chocolate-cream pie instead of a wedding cake? And if so, do I have to share it with anyone?"

He laughed and kissed her again. "Lady, you can have anything you want."

* * * * *